AMERICAN FALLS

American Falls
The Collected Short Stories

BARRY GIFFORD

SEVEN STORIES PRESS

New York ¶ Toronto ¶ London ¶ Sydney

Some of these stories have appeared, several in different form, in the
following publications or in editions issued by the following publishers:
El Ángel de Reforma (Mexico City), The Berkeley Monthly, The Boston Monthly,
Clark City (Livingston, Mont.), Chronicle Books (San Francisco), Crane Hill
(Birmingham, Ala.), Editions Dino Simonett (Zurich), Exquisite Corpse (Baton
Rouge, La.), First Intensity (Lawrence, Kan.), Max (Milan), Sábado de Uno
Masuno (Mexico City), San Francisco magazine, The San Francisco Chronicle,
The San Francisco Examiner, and Zyzzyva.

Seven Stories Press
140 Watts Street
New York NY 10013
http://www.sevenstories.com

In Canada:
Hushion House, 36 Northline Road, Toronto, Ontario M4B 3E2

In the U.K.:
Turnaround Publisher Services Ltd., Unit 3, Olympia Trading Estate,
Coburg Road, Wood Green, London N22 6TZ

In Australia:
Tower Books, 2/17 Rodborough Road, Frenchs Forest NSW 2086

Library of Congress Cataloging-in-Publication Data
Gifford, Barry, 1946-
American Falls : the collected short stories / Barry Gifford.—
A Seven Stories Press 1st ed.
p. cm.
ISBN 1-58322-470-X (Cloth)
1. United States—Social life and customs—20th century—Fiction. I. Title.
PS3557.I283 A6 2002
813'.54—dc21
2002001130
9 8 7 6 5 4 3 2 1

College professors may order examination copies of Seven Stories Press titles
for a free six-month trial period. To order, visit www.sevenstories.com/textbook,
or fax on school letterhead to (212) 226-1411.

Book design by M. Astella Saw

Printed in the U.S.A.

this book is for the boys—
gene,
ray,
and doctor bruce

Contents

"I Wish I'd Made It Up"
A NOTE TO THE READER

On a summer's day in 1957, I was sitting on top of the backrest of a bench next to a ballfield at Green Briar Park in Chicago when for some reason I no longer can remember I thought about how old I would be in the year 2000. The answer was fifty-three, a figure virtually beyond imagining insofar as the possibility of my ever attaining such an age. The millennial year itself likewise eluded serious speculation—at ten I had difficulty contemplating much beyond the very moment. I was shaken from this reverie of the incomprehensible by a kid shouting at me, "Hey, Gif, you're up!"

I am now fully two years older than the fifty-three that seemed so unrealistic as well as unrealizable that afternoon in Green Briar Park forty-four and a half years ago. Turning thirty, or forty, or fifty, did not disturb me. My Uncle Buck, who will be ninety-one this coming May, told me several years ago that according to his research anyone who dies before the age of 120 has died a premature death. About a year ago, he revised this plateau of minimal longevity to 130.

Perhaps he's right. At ninety, Uncle Buck works steadily as a civil engineer and architect, drawing plans for houses and offices, keeping almost as busy as ever. He took off for ten days in November and went fishing out of Progréso, on the Yucatan coast, with a guide only slightly younger than himself. No old men of the sea, Buck reported that they were extremely successful, catching fish every day with nary a mishap.

There's more to the above: the year before, my uncle was in Progréso when he met the guide and arranged to go out fishing with him the next morning. That night he broke his leg and had to be hospitalized. The guide had no telephone, so Buck could not contact him. After one week in the hospital in Progréso, my uncle, using a pair of hand-hewn crutches furnished for him by the husband of one of the nurses in a hospital without doctors, got himself to the closest big town, Mérida, where he literally hopped on a plane back to Tampa, Florida, where he lives. It took quite a while for his leg to heal, but after it did, he returned to Progréso. One morning, about a year later, Buck showed up at the fishing guide's house. "I'm ready to go," Uncle Buck said to the man when he answered the door. The guide stared at my uncle for a few moments, remembered, then said, "Let me get my hat."

It was in the same year, 1957, that I considered the phenomenon of turning fifty, that I began writing stories. My first effort, titled "All in Vain," was about two brothers who fought on opposite sides during the War Between the States. It was about seven pages long, printed on yellow legal paper. My mother threw it out in a cleaning frenzy some years later, so I don't have it for reference, but I do recall that at the end the two boys shot each other and they both died.

I've always considered the short story the most difficult form in which to write. I've written novels, essays, plays, screenplays, poems, songs, even an open libretto, but the short story has always been my favorite, most challenging mode of composition. It seems to me that the story about my uncle and his fishing guide in Mexico is about as perfect a story as there can ever be. I wish I'd made it up. The ones in this book are the best I've been able to make up so far.

BARRY GIFFORD
Christmas 2001

American Falls

The weather wasn't what could be called really cold yet, not in this part of the country, early mid-October in southern Idaho, but it was in the air, that threat locals became aware of almost as soon as the Winnebagos beat their retreat after Labor Day. Yoshiko shivered as she walked the nearly two hundred yards from where the schoolbus dropped her off to the motel. This morning her mother, Maiko, had made her wear her father's old sheepskin coat, the one Toru claimed he had been wearing when he was run over by a train. This was Yoshiko's father's favorite story, one he had told to her and her little brother, Miki, many times, showing them the coat with two black crease marks across the back of it that he insisted were made by the locomotive's wheels. Yoshiko was now thirteen and she knew it would have been impossible for her father to have survived such an accident had the indentations on the coat been made by a train. Miki, at ten, still believed the story. Toru insisted it was true, and told his children he had descended to earth from the Realm of the Immortals, that he would return there only when the Immortals called him back.

"When will that be?" Miki asked.

"When my work is finished," answered Toru.

"You mean running the motel?" said Yoshiko, sarcastically.

"No," said her father, smiling at her feigned insouciance. "When both of you are grown up and well on your way in the world."

Throughout this exchange Maiko kept silent; it was not in her nature to debunk or contradict her husband in front of anyone, especially their children. Privately, however, she chastised him for fostering false beliefs in Yoshiko and Miki.

"They'll really believe you're immortal," she said, "that you're going to live forever."

"Well, perhaps I will," said Toru.

Yoshiko arrived at the motel office just as Al Miller, the postman, pulled up in his green 1957 Chrysler Newport with three dents in the hood he claimed had been made by an eight-point buck that bounced off the car the evening of the late September day he'd bought it. The buck, Al said, had stared at him through the windshield for several moments before sliding off and dashing into the brush. Yoshiko had always meant to ask Al Miller why he'd never had the dents pounded out but she never remembered to do this when she saw him. Al said the deer had eyes like Ava Gardner's.

"Afternoon, Yoshiko," he said, after he'd rolled down his driver's side window. Al held out toward her a small, rolled-up packet of mail bound by a rubber band. "You can save me getting out.

My hip's botherin' me fierce as a wolverine in heat, and if I move sudden my lower back stiffens up."

Al was a short, bald, overweight man in his early fifties. He always had terrible breath from bad cigars so Yoshiko kept an arm's length from him as she accepted the mail packet.

"Thanks, honey. Say hello to your folks for me."

The postman rolled his window back up and drove off.

Yoshiko looked at the mail before going inside. Most of it consisted of advertising flyers and magazines addressed to Blackfoot Motel, Star Route, Highway 30, American Falls, Idaho. There were a couple of business-size envelopes addressed to her father. Nothing for her. Yoshiko had a pen pal in Alexandria, Egypt, named Nazli Mrabet, from whom she was expecting a letter. Each of the students in Yoshiko's eighth grade class at her school in Pocatello, which was twenty-five miles east of American Falls, had pen pals in various parts of the world. Nazli was very curious about the United States of America; she didn't understand, she wrote Yoshiko, how a Japanese girl could be living in a motel in Idaho. Yoshiko explained to Nazli that her grandfather, her father's father, had emigrated from Osaka to Wyoming in 1912 to work on the railroad, and after that had traveled up to Idaho where he had a farm and where her father, Toru, had been born. Toru had met Yoshiko's mother, Maiko, in San Francisco, when he was visiting that city's Nihonmachi, the Japantown closest to Idaho, on a holiday. Together her parents had worked on the farm, then sold it and bought the Blackfoot Motel in American Falls.

Yoshiko had also to explain what a motel was as opposed to a hotel. Even though it was 1965, there was still no such thing as a motor hotel in Egypt, at least not in Alexandria. Perhaps there were motels in Cairo, Nazli wrote, but she couldn't say because she had never been to Cairo. She hoped to go there in a few years, she told Yoshiko, to attend nursing school. Nazli had wanted to be a nurse since she was a little girl, ever since she had visited her father, Ahmed, in a hospital after his left leg had been severely mutilated in a construction accident. The nurses had been so kind and attentive to her father, Nazli said, and had taken such good care of him, that Ahmed did not lose his leg as the doctors feared he might. For now she maintained a doll hospital, and repaired her own and friends' damaged dolls.

Yoshiko entered the motel office, which was also the front door to her family's living quarters. Toru was standing behind the registration desk, reading the previous day's newspaper.

"Hi, Pop," said Yoshiko. "Miki feeling any better?"

Her father looked up at her over his wire-rim reading glasses.

"I think so. Your mother made him stay in bed all day."

As Yoshiko passed through the office, heading towards the "house," she asked, "Any new customers today?"

"Not yet," said Toru, "still early."

Maiko was in the kitchen, cutting vegetables. Yoshiko kissed her mother, who told her not to disturb Miki, that he was asleep. Yoshiko went to her room and closed the door. She was tired, too, having risen at five o'clock that morning to finish her homework from the day before. She had more homework to do now, but she collapsed on her bed without taking off her father's heavy sheepskin coat.

When she woke up it was black outside. She was sweaty and heavy-headed but felt better when she smelled the familiar and pleasant odor of cooking rice coming from the kitchen. Yoshiko got up, took off the coat and went to the bathroom to clean up for dinner. She could hear muffled voices in conversation as she washed her face. As Yoshiko dried herself with a towel, she realized there was a voice she did not recognize talking to her father. This person, a man, thought Yoshiko, spoke with an accent entirely unfamiliar to her. She became curious about the voice, so hastily completed her washing and went to the office. There she saw a black man, not very big, perhaps an inch or two taller than Toru, who was below average height. The man was quite a bit thicker than her father, but Yoshiko sensed those were muscles straining against his powder blue summer sportcoat, not fat. He was in his early to mid-thirties, agreeable to look at, she thought, with a narrow mustache shorn so that it curliecued slightly over the rim of his upper lip like a slinky, dark brown caterpillar.

The man stopped talking when Yoshiko appeared. He stared at her.

"My daughter," said Toru.

Then the man stopped looking at her, said "Thank you" to Yoshiko's father, and walked out of the office through the front door. Maiko emerged from the kitchen and stared after him.

"Who's that, Pop?" asked Yoshiko.

"A customer," he said. "I gave him twenty-nine."

"I've never seen a black person before," said Yoshiko.

"Sure you have," said Toru, "on television."

"That's not the same."

"Why is he here?" asked Maiko.

"I didn't ask him."

"What did he tell you?"

"He wanted a room. I gave him one."

"Maybe he's going to work on the dam," said Yoshiko. "I heard at school the American Falls Dam Company is hiring again."

"Who told you that?"

"Mr. James, my history teacher, told Buddy French that if he didn't have his next book report in on time he might just as well go get one of those new jobs at the dam because his chances of graduating grammar school would be little or none."

"I don't think so," said Toru.

"Buddy French told Mr. James he was going to work as a ranger in the Minidoka woods. Why do you think the black man is here, Pop?"

"He could be a criminal," said Maiko. "From Denver, or Reno."

"I think he's sort of pretty," said Yoshiko.

"Is dinner ready?" asked Toru.

Maiko ducked back into the kitchen. Yoshiko and Toru followed her and found Miki already seated, spooning rice into his mouth. Toru and Yoshiko sat down.

"You must be feeling better," Toru said to his son. "I'm glad."

"Me, too," said Miki, spitting rice onto the table.

"Don't talk with your mouth full," scolded Maiko, as she took her seat.

"What kind of a car is he driving?" asked Yoshiko.

"Chevy Impala," said Toru.

"New?"

"Three years old, 1962. White."

"What kind of car is who driving?" Miki asked.

"A black man is in twenty-nine," said Yoshiko.

"I want to see," said Miki. He slid off his chair and ran out of the kitchen.

"Miki!" shouted Maiko. "Finish your dinner!"

"I'll get him," said Yoshiko, who got up and followed her brother.

Maiko looked at Toru. "Why don't you say something?"

Toru kept eating. "Such as?"

"Get them to behave."

"They behave very well, I think. The soup is delicious."

Miki had left the front door open and Yoshiko stepped out onto the little porch. She could see Miki in front of twenty-nine, checking out the ivory '62 Impala.

"Miki," she said, "come back in. Remember, you're sick."

Miki skipped back and up the steps.

"Not anymore, I'm not," he said, grinning. "That's a pretty sharp car. The license plate is from Illinois."

"Illinois? He must be from Chicago."

Together they went inside, closed the door, and rushed to the registration book, which lay open on the desk.

"What does it say?" asked Miki, as his sister read silently.

"Charles Bone, 225 Arvin Road, Rockford, Illinois."

"Is Rockford, Illinois, a long way from here?"

"A very long way."

Yoshiko and Miki went back into the kitchen and sat down at the table.

"Find out anything interesting?" asked Toru.

"He's Charles Bone from Rockford, Illinois," said Yoshiko, "but you already know."

"That's what he says," said Miki. "He could be making it up."

"It doesn't matter, does it?" said Maiko. "Now finish your dinner."

"Charles Bone is a strange name, don't you think, Pop?" Yoshiko asked.

"Some people might say the same about our names," said Toru. "Maybe where he comes from the name Bone is quite common."

Maiko stood up, picked up her bowls and carried them to the sink.

"I just hope he's not a bad man," she said.

"Bad men need to sleep, too, Mama," said Toru.

Maiko turned on the faucet and began washing dishes.

"He should sleep and go."

Toru laughed. "Don't worry. This man has a good face."

Yoshiko and Miki finished eating, got up with their bowls and put them in the sink.

"I have homework," said Yoshiko.

Miki headed toward the office again.

"Where are you going?" Toru asked him.

"I just want to see," said Miki.

"There's nothing to see," said Maiko. "Miki, you've been sick. Go back to bed."

Miki looked through the curtains on the front window. The Impala was still parked there and a light was on in twenty-nine. Then the light went off.

Toru came and stood next to his son.

"Anything exciting to report?"

"The light in his room just went out."

"Mr. Bone is probably tired from driving."

Toru picked up his son, who was small for his age.

"Your mother is right, you should get back into bed if you're going to school tomorrow."

"Okay, Pop."

Miki put his head down on his father's left shoulder and let him carry him to his room.

Later, when Toru and his wife were in bed, Maiko said, "You spoil them."

"Yes, I do. I spoil them well."

"What does that mean?"

Toru laughed, turned out the light next to his side of the bed, and said, "They'll have good memories of their time with us."

The front door buzzer rang twice at three-thirty in the morning, awakening Toru and Maiko immediately. Before his wife could say anything, Toru was up, putting on his robe and slippers. The buzzer sounded again, twice more.

"Mr. Bone," said Maiko, sitting up.

"Stay here," said her husband.

Toru switched on a light in the kitchen as he walked towards the front office, where he also turned on a lamp. Someone pressed the buzzer once, a long buzz.

Through the glass in the door Toru saw two men wearing dark overcoats and hats. Toru unlocked the dead bolt but left the chain latched, opening the door only as far as the chain allowed.

"Yes?" he said.

"Police," said one of the men, taking out a wallet, flipping it open and displaying a detective's badge, "from Pocatello."

Toru looked at the man's badge. Then the other man took out a wallet and flashed a similar badge.

"I'm Detective Sergeant Foster," said the second man to open his wallet, "and this is Detective Sergeant Poole. May we come in? Sorry to disturb you in the middle of the night, but it's important."

Toru closed the door, unlatched the chain, reopened the door and let the men come inside. They were both tall and wide, much larger than Toru. They stood in the office and looked the place over. The two of them with Toru made the room seem very small.

Toru noticed that one of the men had a large purple birthmark on his right cheek that extended down to his collar. This was the one named Poole.

"Yeah, sorry to disturb you," said Poole. "We wake you up?"

Toru nodded.

"You alone here?" asked Foster.

"No, my wife and children are sleeping. The children are, anyway. My wife is awake."

"Well, sorry," said Foster.

"We're looking for a man," said Poole. "We thought maybe he stopped here."

"A Negro," said the other one, "named Dodge. Elder Dodge."

Poole pulled a 3 x 5 black and white photograph out of a pocket and handed it to Toru.

"That's his picture. Taken a year ago, in San Francisco."

"He might be headed there," said Foster.

Toru took the snapshot and held it under the desk lamp to have a better look, then handed it back to Detective Sergeant Poole.

"You seen him?" asked Poole.

"I don't believe so."

"Don't get too many Negroes up this way," said Foster. "You'd remember a Negro."

"Yes," said Toru.

"Last we knew he was driving a 1958 blue and white Ford Fairlane hardtop," Foster said. "Nevada plates."

"May I ask," said Toru, "what offense, if any, this Mister—"

"Dodge," said Poole, "Elder Dodge. He killed a woman."

"His wife. One of 'em, anyway," said Foster. "In L.A., last March. Shot her in the head and scrammed."

"What makes you think he's around here?" asked Toru.

Poole massaged the purple birthmark on his face.

"Someone spotted him in Twin Falls," he said, "recognized him from a Wanted poster in the post office."

"How can you be certain it was the same man?" said Toru. "To some white people, all Negroes look the same."

Foster stared hard at Toru. "Or Orientals," he said.

"What about Orientals?" asked Toru.

"You could say the same thing, that to some white people all Orientals look the same."

"Perhaps," said Toru.

"Maybe to some Orientals," said Poole, "all white people look the same."

"How about Negroes?" said Foster. "Could be to some of them all Orientals look alike."

Toru waited for the detectives to ask him more questions but they only stood in the dimly lit office glancing around.

"Do you want to see the motel register?" Toru asked.

"All right," said Poole.

Toru went around behind the desk and opened the registration book. Poole examined it.

"Charles Bone," he read aloud. "Rockford, Illinois. He the only one to rent a room today?"

"Yes, sir," said Toru.

"You check his plates? They Illinois plates?"

Toru hesitated a moment before answering, then said, "Yes, one of my employees did."

"That white Chevrolet Impala out there," said Foster.

"Ivory," said Poole.

"Yes," said Toru.

Poole took out a card and placed it on the desk in front of Toru.

"If you run across this male Negro Dodge," he said, "call the number there. Don't let on you know who he is, he's dangerous."

"Armed and dangerous," said Foster.

"I won't," said Toru.

"Call any time," said Poole. "Twenty-four hours."

"I will."

The two detectives again gave the office the once over.

"You're Japanese," Foster said.

"Yes," said Toru. "Japanese-American."

"Born here?" asked Poole.

"My father worked for the Union Pacific in Wyoming. After that he came to Idaho and bought a farm. I was born in Shoshone."

"Worked on the railroad, huh?" said Poole.

Toru nodded.

"How many kids you got?" asked Foster.

"Two," said Toru, "a boy and a girl."

The detectives moved to the door. Foster opened it.

"You ought to have a better lock on this," he said. "Anybody could bust this chain."

"Just kick the door open," said Poole.

"I'll see to it," said Toru. "Thank you."

The two men left the office, Foster first. Poole did not close the door behind him. Toru came around from behind the desk and watched the detectives get into their car and drive away, heading east on 30, towards Pocatello.

Toru closed and locked the door. He went back behind the desk, picked up the telephone receiver and dialed room number twenty-nine. It rang four times before someone picked up.

"Mr. Bone?"

"Who's this?"

"Toru Suzuki, the motel proprietor."

"What time is it?"

"Almost four A.M. I'm sorry to bother you, Mr. Bone, but I thought I should tell you that two detectives were just here looking for a man named Elder Dodge."

"Elder Dodge?"

"Yes, from Los Angeles."

"Mm. What this got to do with me?"

"Perhaps nothing. I'm very sorry to have disturbed you, Mr. Bone."

Toru hung up. He turned off the lamp in the office and went to his bedroom. Maiko was still sitting up in the bed. Toru took off his robe and slippers and got under the covers.

"What did they want?" she asked.

"They were looking for someone."

"Who?"

"A man named Elder Dodge."

"Do you know him?"

"I've never met anyone by that name."

Toru turned out the light next to his side of the bed.

The next morning when Yoshiko and Miki went outside to walk to the bus stop, they noticed that the white Impala was gone.

"Yosh, look," said Miki, "Mr. Bone left really early."

"He must have a long way to drive today," said his sister, walking ahead.

Yoshiko could feel snow in the air. She was glad to be wearing the sheepskin coat.

Wrap It Up

Last night I had dinner with my friend Rocco. We were talking about our respective families, our children, who range collectively in age from three to twenty-eight, and our wives, both past and present. The conversation turned to a discussion of how our various family members deal with disappointment and tragedy, great and small.

Rocco's wife, Vi, his second, is Vietnamese. He told me that recently he saw her crying and asked what was wrong. Vi said that she had been thinking about her cousin and his wife and three children who had not survived their voyage from Vietnam to the Philippines following the end of the war in 1975. Vi and her father, mother and brother had barely survived their own emigration on a separate boat, sailing for a month with only a week's worth of food and water from Haiphong to Subic Bay.

Rocco had not heard the story of Vi's cousin's ordeal before and when he saw how upset his wife was he asked her to tell him what had happened. Vi said that Thai pirates had boarded the ship and demanded that everyone on it hand over to them their gold and jewelry. Vi's cousin told them he had no gold or jewelry, that he and his family had exchanged their valuables for passage. The pirates cut off one of his feet and threw it into the water, attracting sharks. Again the pirates asked for his gold and again he told them he had none. They threw him overboard and made his wife and children watch as the sharks tore his body apart.

The pirates then demanded that Vi's cousin's wife give them her valuables. She said her husband did not lie, they had no gold or jewelry. The pirates then threw her children, all three of them, into the bloody water where they, too, were dismembered by sharks. The woman became hysterical and could not answer the Thai pirates' final demand that she surrender to them her gold and jewelry. In view of the other terrified passengers, she jumped overboard.

Vi stopped crying, Rocco said, and told him that she would now take this terrible memory and put it into a little box and store it in a far corner of her mind and never think about it again. She would always have it with her, Vi said, she would know it was there, but she would not remember it any more.

Rocco told me his head was filled with little boxes, too, the difference being that he couldn't keep from opening them over and over, even when he didn't want to. What about you? he asked.

My mind, I said, is one big open box. The only thing I can't remember is where I put the lid.

A Fair Price

Felice Vano knew he was not really a very good actor but he was not a bad one, either. If he were too good he would not have become a television star in Italy. Ordinary people, the ones who watched the kinds of programs Felice was featured in, identified with him more easily than they would, say, an actor the caliber of Laurence Olivier. Watching Olivier the viewer was aware a performance was taking place; with Felice Vano, the audience—and Vano, as well—understood always that he was merely one of them, pretending to be someone he or they were not and never could be.

Vano thought about his career as he sipped an espresso and looked around at the faces in the bar. Felice liked coming home to Castel Agnese every few months. He especially enjoyed fleeing Rome during October, when the social season was raging. Felice had never cared for parties other than as a necessary evil to endure for the purpose of meeting women. At the moment he didn't care if he ever had a girlfriend again, let alone a wife, of which he had had three. This was not a fact he was proud of, especially since he would not be thirty-four years old for two more months.

Actors, Felice Vano believed, were perhaps the least well-equipped human beings on the planet to lead successful personal lives. They were forever moving around and—even if they were lucky enough to be working at the moment—hustling up their next job. Actors never had the time to find out who they really were. Felice's friend Marcello Ghezzi, who also had been an actor before committing suicide at the age of thirty, six years ago, used to say that every actor should have tattooed on one of his arms the letters IC, for Identity Crisis.

Vano was one of the few among his youthful contemporaries to escape Castel Agnese and its environs. Most of his childhood friends and acquaintances still lived in or around the town and worked in the agricultural industry or services related to the local tourist trade. Castel Agnese was famous for its olive groves and holiday resorts, attracting during the good weather months vacationers from all over the world. Felice's father, now in his early sixties, operated a tobacco shop in the central district assisted by his wife. Felice's mother had during her lifetime never traveled out of the region, and her husband only once, when he had been taken at the age of sixteen to Brindisi to attend the funeral of his father's favorite aunt.

Many times Felice Vano had invited his parents, other relatives and various friends from Castel Agnese to visit him in Rome, but nobody did. All appreciated his offer but even the thought of confronting such a potentially confusing place disconcerted them. Interestingly enough, the very few of Vano's pals who left Castel Agnese did not stop at Rome, or not for very long, anyway. They kept going and were now living in Spain, England, the United States, Australia and Argentina.

Felice had by chance run into Paolo Palantonio, with whom he had gone through school from the age of five to seventeen, in Los Angeles a couple of years before. Paolo was working as a waiter in a restaurant in West Hollywood. He was gay, living with a much older man, a part-time art dealer who had spent fifteen years in prison for forgery and grand larceny. "Dominic's mother is Italian," Paolo told Felice, "from Rome. She's ninety-six years old and sells crucifixes and rosary beads from a stand near the Vatican. Dominic hasn't seen her in almost forty years but we're planning a trip next spring. I hope she'll still be alive."

Felice paid for his coffee and was about to leave the bar when a boy handed him a folded piece of paper. Vano looked at the boy, who was about fourteen years old. The only remarkable feature about his face was a drooping left eyelid. The boy smiled at Felice, then turned and walked out of the bar. Felice unfolded the piece of paper. It was a note written by an unsteady hand:

> We have your car. It is safe. To get it back come to the entrance to the old olive grove on the Garibaldi Road on the side of the Green City where the sun dies at ten o'clock tonight. Bring ten million lire and we will give you back your car. It's a fair price. If you don't believe this is so ask around. Ten o'clock.

Felice ran out of the bar and down the street to where he had
parked his two month-old black BMW convertible. It was gone.
He looked around frantically. He was alone on the street standing
in the space where his car had been.

Ten million lire. He looked at his watch. The bank would
close in fifteen minutes. He could get the ten million or notify
the police. Better to get the money, he decided, then go to the
cops. He started walking towards the bank. Hell, the local mafiosi
probably had a deal with the police, gave them a cut from every
scam. Welcome home, thought Felice. Welcome fucking home.

He took a taxi to the spot, arriving a few minutes before ten.
The taxi driver asked Felice if he wanted him to wait and the
actor hesitated before saying no. Felice figured he could call
another taxi on his cell phone in case the carnappers didn't show.
It was only after the cabdriver had gone that Vano conjured the
possibility that the thieves might just roll him for the cash and
keep the car, too. "I'm really stupid," he said out loud.

"You might be stupid, but you're a hell of a good actor."

Felice Vano made a three-quarter turn to his left toward the
sound of the voice. A short, burly man stood directly at the
entrance to the olive grove. He was wearing a western-style
fringed jacket cut close to his stocky form, a string tie drawn
through a silver-plated steer head, and hand-tooled carnation-red
cowboy boots. Vano's first thought upon seeing the man was to
ask him what movie he thought he was in.

"You brought the money? What we asked?"

Vano nodded. "Where's my car?"

"Follow me," said the burly man, who then disappeared into the olive grove.

Felice had no choice but to follow, doing his best to keep up with the surprisingly fast-moving Pugliese cowboy. The actor tripped repeatedly during this pursuit, futilely attempting to match his guide's nimble movements. After several minutes Felice found himself in a small clearing deep inside the grove. He stopped, stood still and attempted to regain his breath. He saw his car, on either side of which stood a man, one of whom was the cowboy.

"You see," said this man, who leaned against the driver's door of the BMW, "it's in perfect condition. Take a look for yourself."

Felice Vano moved a few steps closer, then stopped again. The moon was almost full, reflecting off the car's hood as if it were a body of calm black water. Vano saw that the men closely resembled one another and that both of them were smiling. He wondered if they were carrying guns.

"Giovanni's telling the truth," said the man who was leaning against the passenger side. "We didn't put more than ten or twelve kilometers on it."

"Did you ask him if he brought the ten million?" the second man asked the first.

"He told me he's got it."

"Put the money on the hood," the second man instructed.

Vano was suddenly seized by the thought that they intended

to murder him even if he paid the ransom. He stepped forward, removed two envelopes from a pocket of his jacket and placed them on the car.

"There's five million in each one," he said.

The burly men each picked up an envelope, opened it and counted the bills. When they had completed counting they stuffed the bills back into the envelopes and folded them into their coat pockets.

"It's a fair price," said Giovanni.

"A very good price," said the second man. "We're honest here in Castel Agnese. Ask anyone in the region."

"Massimo's word is famous," said Giovanni. "When he speaks it's as if God's shepherd gathered all doubts and lies together and herded them off a cliff."

To this Felice had only one response.

"Where are the keys?"

"In the ignition," said Massimo.

"Is it all right if I go now?" asked Vano.

"Of course," said Giovanni.

"As you like," said Massimo. "It's your car."

Felice walked to the driver's side and Giovanni opened the door for him.

"You're really a wonderful actor," he said.

"Thanks," Felice said, and got into the car. He started it up.

Massimo leaned through the passenger side window and said, "We're great admirers of your work here in Castel Agnese.

Everyone in the town is very proud of you. What was the name of that television show you were in a couple of years ago? The one where you played a former police detective who'd been thrown off the force for being drunk on duty but who kept on solving crimes anyway."

"Musso's Case."

"You were Tommy Musso," said Giovanni.

"That was the character's name."

"I mean," Giovanni said, "you really were Tommy Musso."

"Tommy Musso will always be you," said Massimo, "that's what Giovanni means. Nobody else could be him."

"Absolutely," said Giovanni, "the public would never accept another actor in the role. Tommy Musso is you and you're him, that's it."

"I'll go now," said Felice, "if it's all right."

"Sure, of course, go," said Massimo. "But listen, do us a favor."

Felice looked at Massimo but it was Giovanni who spoke.

"How about giving us a ride?" he said.

"It's a long way back," said Massimo. "We can call a taxi on the cell but who knows how long it'll take or if he'll even come. What do you say?"

Why didn't one of them drive a second car out here? thought Felice.

"Get in," he said.

Massimo climbed in next to Vano and Giovanni got in the back.

"How do I get out of the grove?"

"That way," Massimo said, pointing a finger. "Just drive, we'll tell you where to go."

When they were on the road toward the center of Castel Agnese Giovanni leaned forward and said, "Our families are having a little party tonight, kind of a celebration, you know. I'm sure everyone would like to meet you."

"I know my wife and mother would be thrilled," said Massimo. "They're great fans of yours."

"And my great-aunt Antonella," said Giovanni, "she's eighty-six. She thinks you're more handsome than Clark Gable was."

"Gary Cooper," said Massimo. "Antonella always says Gary Cooper."

"Both of them," Giovanni said, "nothing compared to Felice Vano."

"Felice," said Massimo, "you've got to come in for a moment, just to be kind to these ladies, to be polite."

Felice flinched. "Polite?"

"The world being the way it is," said Massimo, "they might not have the opportunity again."

"How do you see the world?" asked Felice.

"You know, unpredictable."

Felice followed the mens' directions and within ten minutes had parked the car in front of a large old yellow house. Massimo and Giovanni got out on the passenger side.

"Come on," Giovanni said, "just for a moment or two. You'll be making some little people happier than you can imagine."

While driving away from the olive grove Vano had decided to drop off the men and continue straight to the police station; but now, absurd as it seemed, he knew he would accompany Massimo and Giovanni into the house.

"Did you get the money?" a woman of about sixty with a blue turban wrapped around her head asked Massimo as he came first through the door. Immediately behind him was Felice Vano, then Giovanni.

"We did, Mama. Everything went perfectly."

"He didn't go to the police?"

"No, Mama. Look, here he is, just to say hello to the family."

Massimo's mother clasped her hands against her cheeks and shouted, "It's him! It's really him! Felice Vano, the great actor, in our house!"

She grabbed one of Felice's hands and clutched it to her chest, yanking him toward her as she did so, pressing her massive breasts against his abdomen.

"Mama, be careful with the man!"

"Tell me, Signor Vano," she implored, "how much did you pay?"

By now a dozen or more people had gathered around and behind Massimo's mother. Felice looked at their curious, eager faces and wanted to run. Standing directly behind him, however, were Giovanni and Massimo.

"Ten million lire," said Felice.

"Ah! A fair price!" exclaimed Massimo's mother. Her wide,

square face was contorted into a smile that resembled a rumpled bedsheet. Felice was suddenly frightened by the thought that she was going to kiss him and swallow him in the process.

"A very fair price," repeated someone behind Massimo's mother.

Others nodded their heads as they murmured their assent.

Massimo came forward and extracted Felice from his mother's python-like arms, then guided him toward a younger version of the same woman.

"This is my wife, Gabriella," said Massimo. "Gabriellina, meet Felice Vano, the best actor ever to be born in Castel Agnese."

Gabriella brushed Felice's right hand with a wet palm.

"It's a pleasure to meet you," he said.

Massimo's wife suddenly sprang up and directly at Felice's face like an Egyptian cobra, kissing him between his eyes. She drew back, shuddering. Tears streamed down her cheeks. Felice was shocked, mystified and horrified all at the same time. Gabriella buried her head in her husband's chest.

Giovanni took Felice's left arm. "I want you to meet my great-aunt," he said. "Remember, I told you about her."

Felice glided along in Giovanni's embrace. They stopped in front of an ancient, tiny woman who was sitting in a flat-bottomed, high-backed wooden chair. She seemed to be asleep.

"Antonella," Giovanni half-shouted, "look who's here!"

The wizened old lady opened her two enormous black eyes and stared directly into Felice's. He could hardly bear the ferocity of her gaze. Inside this atrophied body, he realized, there thrived a still-terrible beast.

"How much did they ask to get back the car?" crowed Antonella.

"Ten million," answered Felice.

"A fair price," she said, half-closing her ferocious eyes. Antonella flashed them again for a second and croaked, "We're honest people here," before falling back to sleep.

Felice straightened and extricated himself from Giovanni's hold.

"I've got to be going," he said.

Giovanni nodded and grinned. He extended his right hand and shook Felice's.

"You're always welcome in this house."

Massimo came over.

"Felice's leaving," said Giovanni.

"Have a glass of wine," Massimo said. "Bat some salsiccia."

"No, thanks," said Felice.

Massimo grabbed Felice's hand. "Thank you for coming;" he said. "It's really meant a lot to us, to all of us. If you ever need anything in Castel Agnese—anything—let us know."

Felice nodded and started for the front door but Massimo tightened his grip on the actor's hand.

"Promise you will," said Massimo.

He looked into Massimo's eyes. Antonella, Felice realized, was Massimo's grandmother.

"I will," he said.

My Last Martini

The bar of the Hotel Luneau in Paris is a popular meeting place, especially in the late afternoon and early evening. There is a rather ordinary walnut bar with eight stools and brass footrest, but the charming features of the place are the seven maroon leather banquettes that form a half-circle facing the bar, and the three Marie Antoinette chandeliers with dim plum bulbs that convey the impression of a first-class cruise ship's lounge. The atmosphere is, therefore, both convivial and intimate. Patrons sit alone, reading, smoking, or merely gazing around; occasionally there are groups of three or four, but most common are the couples: The Luneau bar is a favorite rendezvous of lovers.

It was there that I was recently told a remarkable story by a complete stranger, a woman I had never seen before nor expect to see again, except by chance. I had met my friend Sharif, as I do most every Wednesday evening at about six-thirty when we're both in town. Sharif is a businessman in his mid-sixties, his businesses being oil and real estate. He keeps apartments in Paris and Houston, and a house in Algiers that is, apparently, quite palatial.

I can't say for certain since I've never been to Algiers, though Sharif has invited me a dozen times to visit. Sharif thinks I don't accept his invitations because I'm afraid the fundamentalist terrorists might slit my throat. Seeing as how I am a white, beardless male, I cannot discount this as a possibility, but the real truth is that I just plain hate to travel.

On this particular evening, Sharif had an early dinner date with another friend, so we spent perhaps forty-five minutes together, during which time we each consumed two martinis and a plate of olives. I believe our conversation concerned the American government's policy of limiting individual companies' investment in Iranian oil to twenty million dollars, and the benefits this has bestowed upon other countries; and the upcoming Prix de l'Arc de Triomphe. Sharif thought the Americans' approach to Iran impossibly parochial, and predicted that Hélissio would take the Arc. I could not dispute him on the oil issue, but I felt that Peintre Célèbre, the American horse, stood a hell of a chance.

After Sharif had gone, I sat quietly, surveying the scene, savoring the dregs of my second martini. Two martinis don't ordinarily affect me other than to provide a feeling of false elation that I treasure for the thirty or so minutes it lasts. I rarely exceed my usual limit of two, however; an excess of elation, I've found, puts the world around me in a light so unflattering that I've been tempted once or twice to make an attempt at extinguishing it. For some reason, when the waiter came by to collect the tab, I

astonished myself by ordering a third. The waiter nodded and
headed back to the bar.

"Do you mind if I join you?" The voice came from an occu-
pant of the booth to my left.

I looked over and saw an attractive dark-haired woman in
her mid-thirties. She was holding a half-filled martini glass in
her right hand.

"I heard you order a martini," she said, "and I thought you
might be someone I could talk to."

By the time she'd finished this sentence, the woman had slid
out of her booth and taken the place of Sharif in mine.

"By all means," I responded.

I studied her as closely as was possible in the muted light. She
was even better looking than I first thought. She wore her chest-
nut hair up, with modest bangs. Her eyes were the same color as
her hair. Only her teeth were imperfect, deeply stained by tobacco. She did not, however, light a cigarette while we were together. The waiter arrived with my martini.

"Would you like another?" I asked.

"Thank you, I would."

I passed this information along to the waiter and he went
away. I was impressed that she did not feel the need to guzzle
the remainder of the drink she kept in her hand, at which I
inadvertently glanced.

"You're a martini man," she said, "you know they're not to
be rushed."

I settled back and watched her take a sip. The toothpick and olive were still in the glass. She didn't say anything else until after the waiter had come and gone again, leaving a fresh martini in front of her. She smiled at me. Her teeth were almost red. Now she downed the last of the martini she'd brought with her, punctuating it by sliding the impaled olive off the toothpick using only the tip of her tongue. In the peculiar light of the Luneau bar, the hue of her tongue matched that of her teeth. She chewed the olive with her eyes closed, then dropped the toothpick back into the glass.

When she'd finished off the olive, she reopened her eyes and said, "Two is my limit. Martinis, that is, not olives."

She pointed with a black fingernail to the drink awaiting her.

"This," she said, with a puma's smile, "will be my third."

I nodded at the glass in front of me.

"Mine, too."

She picked hers up and held it out toward me. I did likewise.

"Santé," she said.

"Santé," I repeated.

We sipped. Remarkably, mine was still very cold.

"Are you Italian?" I asked, though we were speaking French.

"My mother is from Roma."

"And your father?"

"From the country. But he was not pure Italian. He was half-Polish."

"Dead?"

"Yes."

"I'm sure you favor your mother."

She smiled again but quickly cut it off.

"Look," she said, "you must think I'm a bit forward, if not crazy. But I want you to know, I'm not a working girl."

"It wouldn't matter to me if you were, since I'm not at present in the market."

"So. I said I thought you were someone I could talk to. I hope you are, because I have a story I'd like to tell."

"I'm in no particular hurry," I said. "It's a slow night."

"Good. My grandmother, my father's mother, had eight children, six boys and two girls. My father was the third oldest. When she married, she was sixteen years old, a virgin. She lived in a small village in Tuscany. The man to whom she was given in marriage by her parents could not make love. This, of course, she had not known before the marriage."

"Was it annulled?"

"No, impossible. In my grandmother's village, a marriage was forever."

She took a long sip of her martini. I did the same with mine.

"My grandmother was very upset by this, since she wanted to have many children."

"I can barely imagine," I said.

"She made her husband, who was a farmer, ask his Polish worker, who lived in a room underneath the house, below ground, to make love to her. It was this Pole who was the father of my father and his five brothers and two sisters."

"Who knew beside your grandmother and her husband and the Pole?"

"Nobody, until many years later. The Pole would take a broomstick and poke the end of the handle against the ceiling of his underground room to let my grandmother know when he wanted to make love to her."

I swallowed half of what was left of my martini.

"What a remarkable circumstance," I said.

"My father found out when he was twenty-two years old, after my grandmother's husband had died."

"Your grandmother told him?"

"Yes. It was accidental, perhaps. He had done something she didn't like and she cursed him, calling him a dumb Polish bastard. Of course she'd cursed him many times before, but she'd never called him a dumb Polish bastard, and he asked her why she'd said that particular thing."

"And she confessed."

"Yes, it all came out. She cried bitterly and told my father how she had hated both her husband and his Polish worker. She did it to have a family, but finally one night when the Pole banged his broom handle against her floor, she refused to answer. The next morning, when her husband was ready to work, the Pole was gone. He disappeared and nobody in the family ever saw him again."

"How did this news affect your father and the others?"

"My father left for Roma the same day. He rarely saw his

mother after that. It was my mother who took me and my sister and brother to see our grandmother. My father was a terrible womanizer, going from girl to girl always. My mother was quite an unhappy woman."

"But she stayed with your father."

"Until two years before he died. Then he was living with another woman."

Both of us finished our drinks. The woman suddenly leaned over and kissed me full on the lips, a cold martini kiss.

"I'm glad I was right," she said.

"About?"

"Your being a good listener. Often when I have the need to talk, it's difficult to find someone, and I've no use for the church."

She withdrew from the booth, stood for a moment looking at me, then walked away. The waiter came over.

"Another martini, sir?" he asked.

"No," I said, pointing to my empty glass, "this one was definitely my last."

Cat Women
of Rome

I like to walk at night. By myself, usually, late. The other evening when I turned the corner from Via Clitunno onto Via Reno, there was a woman of advanced middle age, perhaps sixty or sixty-five, I guessed, sitting alone on a doorstep in front of a house feeding a dozen or more cats by hand. She smiled at me as I passed, a small, gray, big-nosed lady with charcoal half-moons lurking beneath narrow, sceptre-shaped eyes.

In Rome, these women who feed stray cats, of which there are certainly tens if not hundreds of thousands, are called gattare, cat women. This particular gattare was well-dressed, clean-looking, and displayed no obvious signs of mental illness. Many of the cat women are to some degree disturbed; they speak discourteously, even obscenely to passersby, cursing them for any manner or number of crimes perpetrated against them or the world at large.

In New York, there are, of course, hundreds of men and women who spend a significant portion of their time tossing popcorn or breadcrumbs to pigeons in the parks. The Roman benefactors of felines are almost entirely female and do not limit themselves to the parks which in this city are numerous and inhabited by countless cats. Most of the gattare I've encountered have been like the woman on Via Reno, ensconced in street shadows, nocturnal companions to these legions of peripatetic Egyptian progeny.

The woman whispered soothingly to her furry minions as she doled out to them what appeared to be carefully cut up bite-size pieces of chicken and cheese. As I bisected the space between the majority of them and their benefactress, the variegated gatti wove warily in chiaroscuro, unhurriedly avoiding me, reluctant to be removed substantially from the source of their repast. Several steps past the feeding perimeter, I heard a voice, undoubtedly the cat woman's, call out, "Ma ghevvoi?" Roman dialect for "What do you want?" I turned around and stared back through treebranch shadows shifting and tilting in mottled moonlight. The woman's back was toward me and the cats were clustered before her, stepping on her feet, masticating greedily. Their guttural growls and squeals pierced the summer air as precisely as unseen spears whistle through jungle gloom.

Had the question been meant for me? Or had the gattara directed it to one of her mewling horde? I turned again and continued walking. What did I want? I'd been asking myself this for years.

It's early morning now. Last night I again encountered, entirely on purpose; the cat woman of Via Reno. She grinned at me, as before, and when I asked if she minded my sitting down next to her on the step, she smiled and shook her head. At first the felines semi-circling on the sidewalk kept a cautious distance from me, but they soon realized my presence was not interfering with their partaking of the gattara's largesse and speedily resumed their rotation.

The first thing I noticed after a few minutes' observation was that there was an orderly, if not organized aspect to these cats' actions. Not being a particular student of animal behavior, I am unqualified to say whether the alpha males dominated the pro-ceedings. I did notice that quite a few of the smaller cats seemed to be getting their share as readily as, or even moreso than some of the larger beasts, many of whom were quite savage in their approach and execution.

The cat woman's name was Lucia. She told me she was born in the south, in Reggio Calabria, but her family moved when she was six years old to Rome, where she had lived for the last sixty years. Lucia's voice was a strong, raspy whisper, an insistent, susurrant sound that had the effect on me of provoking rather than inviting the listener to pay strict attention to her words.

Lucia would not tell me about her life "before the cats," as she called it. She'd been with them virtually every night for the past ten years, even in the most inclement weather. "They depend on me," Lucia said. "To disappoint them would lead me to madness."

I thought this last remark curious and I asked her to clarify herself.

"I'll tell you one episode from before. When I was a little girl,

twelve years old, I accompanied my father, who was an opthamol-
ogist, on a trip to Mongolia. He traveled as part of a medical expe-
dition sponsored by the Italian government to dispense ocular
care unavailable to the Mongolians in their own land. One
evening at a dinner in Ulan Bator, two Mongolian women started
laughing in response to something my father had said. They
stopped laughing long enough to ask him, through a translator, to
repeat what he had told them. He did, his words were conveyed
to them by the translator, and again they were seized by parox-
ysms of laughter. They laughed for a full minute or two in a kind
of gentle, quiet way before regaining their composure.

"After dinner, when my father and I were preparing for bed, I
asked him what had caused these women to react in such a way.
He told me that during the course of their conversation he had
mentioned suicide. I knew what suicide was and I didn't understand why they would have laughed. 'They had never heard of
suicide,' my father said. 'I had to explain it to them. They found
the very idea of a person taking his own life so strange they could
not believe it. They thought this was some bizarre invention on
my part. When I elaborated on the concept, the women were
overwhelmed at the absurdity of such a thing. They said a
Mongolian would never have thought of the possibility. That
there were people in Europe who killed themselves was beyond
their imagination.'

"In the days that followed—I believe we remained in
Mongolia for two weeks—whenever these two women were

around, they whispered to other women and pointed at my father, after which they all invariably broke into astonished laughter that sometimes lasted for several minutes. The way they laughed, as I said, was almost silent, bending forward and holding their stomachs and covering their mouths. I knew it was the idea of suicide that was causing this mirth. They were so beautiful, these leathery brown women swathed in black, when they laughed. I'll never forget them."

This was all very interesting, I told Lucia, but what did the Mongolian women's reaction to discovering that there were people in the world who murdered themselves have to do with her devotion to the street cats of Rome?

"They laugh, too," Lucia said, as she finger-fed her feral friends. "They are as amused and mystified by human behavior as the Mongolians were by the Europeans a half-century ago. I would destroy myself before I would betray the cats."

"What if another person appeared on the same street and began feeding the cats?" I asked. "What if the cats abandoned you for another?"

She screwed up her eyes, then closed them, and began to laugh, bending forward and back, an almost silent, gentle laughter that continued for a full minute or two. The cats nibbled her fingers, her hands and wrists, biting her until she ceased laughing and resumed feeding them.

Romántica

Yolanda had a thumbnail-size scar high on her left cheek. When Danny inquired about it she turned sullen and the pink mark became crimson. A shudder, visible to Danny, passed through the length of her body, concluding with a brief facial twist and audible soft gasp. At the moment, the two were semi-entwined, standing under a xanthic desert moon in front of Yolanda's Airstream in East Bakersfield.

"You know what day this is?" asked Yolanda.

"February 29th," he said. "Had a extra day before rent's due."

"El día de Santa Niña de las Putas, the patron saint of Satan's prisoners. It comes only when there's a second full moon in the month on the final day of February in a leap year."

"Knew about the blue moon. Never heard of Satan's prisoners, though."

"Those are souls sold to Satan during the person's lifetime. People who reformed before their death and tried to undo the deal."

Danny disentwined himself, lit a Lucky, inhaled, coughed. The night air felt chilly now that he wasn't pressed against

Yolanda. He rubbed his hands together then shoved them into his pants pockets, letting the cigarette dangle from between his lips.

"Who was Santa Niña?" he mumbled.

"A romántica, like me, born in Jalisco. Her father had bargained with the devil in order to save the life of his wife, who was dying from a cancer. Satan told him his wife would live only if the man promised also the souls of his three sons."

"Not the daughter?"

"Niña was not yet born. She was the youngest of four children. The father was horrified to do this but consented, thinking that later he could persuade Satan not to take his sons. The mother recovered and, of course, no matter how passionately her husband begged, the devil would not relent. The thought that he and his sons were doomed to hell destroyed the poor man, and he died of grief soon after the birth of his daughter."

"Did the mother know about this deal?"

"Not until her husband confessed on his deathbed. When Niña was twelve years old her brothers were killed when a donkey cart in which they were riding broke its axle on a steep mountain road and crashed with the donkey to the bottom of a ravine. Niña's mother then told her about the fate of the boys' souls, so the girl vowed to save them and her father."

Danny spat out the cigarette. "Did she?"

"Yes. That night she called to Satan, telling him she could not live without her brothers, that she wanted to join them immediately. When Satan appeared she took his hand and allowed him to lead her to hell, where she became his mistress."

Suddenly Danny no longer felt the cold. Yolanda had put on a tape of old rock and roll songs in the trailer. Chuck Willis's "Betty and Dupree" was playing. Chuck sang. "Dupree told Betty, I'll buy you anything."

"Satan's attachment to Niña was soon complete," said Yolanda. "She beguiled him in ways even the King of Cruelty had never imagined. In this way was it possible for her to gain a kind of power over the devil and convince him to allow her father and brothers to pass out of hell and enter into the Kingdom of Heaven. Niña, of course, had to remain in hell as Satan's whore. It is the prostitutes who honor her on this, the rarest of days, for her sacrifice."

"Saint Niña of the Whores."

"Our own and only. This is the one day no whore should feel ashamed in the eyes of God."

"But what about your scar? How did you get it?"

"After I made it with a man for money for the first time I cut myself on the face with a sharp edge of a rock."

"But why? You were so beautiful. You still are."

"To never be so beautiful again. I was marked inside and out."

Danny embraced her. "My poor Yolanda."

She pulled away and glared at him. "No," she said, "there is nothing about me that is poor."

Danny sat in his shorts looking out at the sand hills to the south-east. The day was fading fast. He lit a Lucky and listened to the long, lugubrious, wobbly whistle of the southbound Hi-Ball. Danny had grown used to this scorching cry from the evening freight. "La Expresa tristeza" the locals called it, or "El Tormento." Every day at 6:56 P.M., they said, la horca del diablo—the devil's pitchfork—was driven a bit deeper into the soul. Danny had begun to believe it, expecting but never quite being prepared for the whistle. He was always taken by surprise.

Waiting for Yolanda was not easy for him. As a child Danny had often accompanied his daddy. Big Danny, on his rounds of the Bakersfield area bars. While Big Danny drank and caroused. Danny was made to sit outside on the curb or in the pickup, sometimes for hours at a time, staring at and being stared at by passersby. Sometimes kids picked fights with him, older kids, and Danny often had to run away and sneak back later, hoping that his father had not left him behind. Big Danny's juerga inevitably ended in a brawl. Danny's abiding mental picture of his daddy—who died of a stab wound to the chest when Danny was sixteen—was Big Danny's bloodied face as he stumbled out of some dive. Danny always told people who asked that his daddy had died from a heart attack. He never told them that Big Danny's heart had been attacked with a blade wielded by a drunken coyote in a shitkicker bar called Rowdy Dave's Dream of Paradise.

Danny's mother, Lee Ella, had died from pneumonia when the boy was four. He barely remembered her. Big Danny, who stood four foot eleven and one-quarter inch without his boots, was a legendary figure on the midget rodeo circuit from Chula Vista to San Jose. His best event, before alcoholism forced him to quit, had been bull riding. Big Danny made his bones beating the clock at Stockton on a terrible beast named Nasty At Night. When he wasn't rodeoing, Big Danny worked construction and did odd jobs. Danny had been on his own since his daddy's death. Until his infatuation with Yolanda Rios, he'd kept clear of attachments. Now he was waiting again.

Danny decided to fortify himself before having it out with Yolanda. He drove out past Famoso and stopped at a bar named El Lagarto Tuerto. Danny's left bootheel hit the sand just as a corona discharge gyrated onto a telephone pole next to the highway. Danny ducked back into his Cutlass as he watched St. Elmo's fire roll along the line like an acrobat riding a bicycle on a high wire. The blue-white lightning ball danced daintily on its silent path for several seconds, then disappeared as rapidly as it had come, leaving only a path of mist in its wake. There had been no thunder or noise other than a faint hiss following the sphere's decay.

Danny waited a few moments before again attempting to disembark. He recalled having read in UFO Monthly, a magazine he'd found lying around Chifla Miguel's Chop Shop, that ball lightning was often misidentified as a spaceship. In fact, it was gas or air behaving in an unusual way, powered perhaps by a high-frequency electro-magnetic field or focused cosmic ray particles. As he lowered his leg again to the ground, Danny heard thunder, and he hurried toward the bar before the rain came. Thunderstorms, he knew, functioned as batteries to keep the earth charged negatively and the atmosphere charged positively.

Danny reached the entrance just as several tons of water hit the earth in his immediate vicinity. As far as it being a good or bad omen, he couldn't tell. Danny only hoped that God knew what He was doing, because he wasn't too sure about himself.

There were only two customers inside, both seated on barstools since there were no tables and chairs. Danny stood at the bar for two minutes but no bartender appeared. He turned to the patron nearest to him and was about to ask if someone were working, but the man was sound asleep, snoring with his head resting on his arms on the counter. Danny shifted his attention to a black-bearded man at the opposite end who sat staring at the label of a beer bottle in front of him.

"Hey, pardner," Danny said, "anybody servin'?"

The man did not respond.

"Hey, buddy: Amigo! I asked, anybody work here?"

The customer so addressed promptly fell off of his barstool, out of Danny's sight.

"Jesus, what a place," he said.

He could hear the storm raging outside, loud thunder and heavy rain. Nevertheless, Danny turned toward the door.

"Welcome to the One-Eyed Lizard!" boomed a voice behind him.

Danny did a one-eighty and saw a white-haired woman who stood well over six feet tall. She had a hawk nose and eyes that went with it. The woman was wearing a checkered shirt and blue-jeans held up by red suspenders spread wide by her enormous bosom. Danny pegged her age at fifty-five, give or take a few.

"You want a drink or not?" she barked.

Danny returned to the bar. "I didn't see anybody workin'."

"You see someone now. What'll it be?"

"Negra Modelo, I guess."

The large woman squinted, taking a closer look at him.

"You're a cloudy boy, all right."

"Cloudy?"

"Not too certain about yourself."

She produced a bottle of beer, cracked it open, and placed it on the bar in front of Danny, where it foamed over on the counter.

"How can you tell?" he asked.

The woman snorted. "There's even more I can't—won't—tell ya. I've got the gift."

"The gift?"

"The gift of seein' both the present and the future at the same time. See my eyes?"

Danny stared at them. Both were pale blue with extraordinary dilated pupils.

"A seer, son. Same as Amos, Asaph, Gad, Heman, Samuel, and Zadok. You heard of them, ain't ya?"

"No, ma'am."

"What do you do, boy?"

"Work on cars. Race 'em, too."

She stared directly at Danny, leaning forward, her large hands pressing down hard on the bar. Her right eye wandered, jerked, rolled around. Danny watched it move.

"Your right eye the one sees the future?"

The woman leaned back. Her eye calmed down.

"Break thou the arm of the wicked and the evil man," she said. "Seek out his wickedness till thou find none."

"Yes, ma'am."

"Drink up and go."

Danny took a long swig from the bottle, set it back down on the counter, and pulled a dollar from his pocket.

"No charge," the woman said. "Go your way. I send you forth as a lamb among wolves."

Danny ran through the rain to his car, got in, and sat there thinking about what the woman had said. Suddenly, a single vertical bolt of cloud-to-ground lightning exited as a bright pink spot atop the thunderhead. It struck the tin roof of El Lagarto Tuerto, igniting the Cutlass's engine. Danny sat in the idling automobile, trembling. It was time to find Yolanda.

The Old Days

Felix Martucci took his time getting off the plane. He had to because of the instability of his left knee, which had been replaced three months before, but he also enjoyed the feeling, the luxury of moving leisurely and the general latitude given by others to a person of a certain age. Felix Martucci would be eighty-four years old in six weeks, a fact that he found difficult to entirely comprehend. Each morning when he looked at his face in the mirror he asked himself, "Who is that guy?"

Martucci had never been indolent, nor had he been a nervous type. His calm but purposeful demeanor was always a plus. Men trusted him, and in his business—or what formerly had been his business—this was the finest attribute of all. To be feared was not without benefits, but trust, as Benny Pickles put it, was the grandfather of respect. Benny Pickles, poor man, may he rest in peace. Gone now how many years? Five? Six? Everybody was gone, just about, except himself. Whoever else was still alive wasn't worth a thought.

Felix stepped carefully to the exit and paused briefly, closing his eyes before emerging onto the platform of the stairway. He took a deep breath and opened his eyes, looking out at Havana for the first time in forty years. Strange, he thought, not to have a strong feeling of any kind at this moment. The air was sultry but not quite as warm as he had expected it to be. A flight steward took his arm, a young man. Felix sized him up.

"May I be of assistance, sir? The stairs are a little wet."

In the old days, thought Felix, it would have been a pretty young woman holding his elbow. This guy was probably a fag, but what the hell. Junie's boy, Marty, was a fag, and he was a pretty good kid, a good grandson. It didn't matter anymore, not much did. Fuck the old days, too. He hated that expression.

Felix negotiated the stairs without slipping. He wondered if the steward knew who he was, that he'd been responsible for the premature demise of more than a few men—not that they hadn't earned their deaths—whether he would handle the elderly gentleman in such a tender fashion.

Back in the fifties, Felix recalled, there was always a car to meet him on the tarmac next to the plane, usually a late-model convertible. Today he took a taxi, a 1957 Chevy Bel Air held together by wire and spit. There had to be some marvelous automobile mechanics in Cuba, able to keep these ancient vehicles percolating.

He would stay at the Hotel Nacional, as he had always done. In Miami, Felix preferred the Biltmore, in the Gables. Both hotels had been designed by the same man. People knew what style and elegance were back then. Just look at Vegas to see what things have come to, if you can do it and keep from puking. Fat parents with fat kids eating ice cream cones, all of them wearing shorts. Casinos in shopping malls with animal acts, for God's sake.

Felix Martucci sat on the terrace smoking a Cohiba, the only thing he could thank Castro for creating. Felix didn't know if the one he was smoking was the real goods or not, but it tasted. Since his second heart attack he hadn't touched tobacco or alcohol. Now he sipped a mojito and puffed away. It wouldn't be so terrible, he figured, to die in this place, a city filled with good memories for him. The government here had finally wised up and started behaving like the Syndicate. Plenty of new hotels and cheap hookers were bringing in the suckers, mostly from Europe and Canada, of course, but those people could spend too.

Once at the Riviera with Lipsky a made guy out of Cleveland named Nicky Pants tried to cut a deal for the docking charges. Lipsky wanted to know what he had to offer and Nicky Pants said the casino boat on Lake Erie. There wasn't any casino boat on Lake Erie. What was he talking about? Lipsky could put one there and this Nicky Pants would keep it safe. Lipsky didn't know how an escaped mental patient got in the room. Nicky Pants raised his voice. The next morning he was found tied to a piling, his legs bitten to the bone by barracudas. Felix had been happy to do a service for Lipsky. The man made everything go in Havana and Martucci went with it.

The water still looked pretty good. There didn't used to be so many young people hanging around on the streets. At least he didn't think so. What a shame the place had to go to the dogs, a real waste. It wasn't just the real estate, either; it was the people. They liked a good time. Felix smiled at the memory of watching a golden-skinned woman with big black eyes wearing only a live snake while she danced at the Tropicana. The snake's head rested on her left breast, its tongue flicking out and in in time to the music, its only moving part. Now that was an act. Maybe in Asia it's done, but back then, only in Cuba.

There was another reason Felix Martucci had come to Havana, one aside from nostalgia. He had a son here. The boy, if he was alive, would be forty-two years old. Not a boy anymore. The same age Felix was when he was born. His name was Felix, too; at least it had been the last time he'd seen him. Little Felix was two then, a coffee-colored kid with wild, wavy black hair like his father had when he was young. Where his son's mother was now Martucci had no clue. She might be dead, of course. Her name was Sonya Despacio, and she'd been twenty-four when they'd met, a dancer at the Hi-Hat, one of Benedetti's clubs.

Martucci had rarely thought about this son over the years. He had enjoyed a decent enough if not terribly close relationship with his three daughters and six grandchildren. Until she died a year ago, Anna's life revolved around the kids and their lives. Felix pretty much stayed out of the fray. Since Anna's passing after fifty-one years of marriage, Felix had stayed mostly to himself, content to allow the housekeeper prepare meals and answer the telephone. He watched ball games, read mystery novels, and played cards once or twice a week with the few cronies he had left.

The thought to visit Havana and the remote possibility of finding Little Felix energized him. But now that he was here, Martucci really wasn't sure what to do. Getting to Cuba had been simple: He flew to Cancún, Mexico, and from there to Havana. Nobody blinked an eye at the several Americans, including himself, making the trip despite the United States government's prohibition on travel to the island. Felix just made certain his passport wasn't stamped, though he couldn't have cared less about getting into trouble. What could anybody, even the government, do to an octogenarian who'd had two heart attacks in the past two years?

Sonya was engaged to be married when Felix met her. They spent a week together at Varadero Beach in a villa Lipsky kept there. She was dark-skinned except for light patches under her arms and behind her knees. At certain moments parts of her looked almost blue, especially after she'd been in the sun for an extended period of time. Felix told her she reminded him of some exotic tropical fish. Sonya's brown eyes had bright yellow flames in them that appeared to leap out when she became particularly excited. Felix described them once as two flares igniting simultaneously, penetrating his soul in a way nobody else ever had. He knew Sonya had never loved him, and Felix was not sure he had ever loved her. Nevertheless, he attached a significance to their relationship that was unique in his experience.

Oddly enough for Felix Martucci, he felt a certain amount of guilt for having virtually abandoned Sonya Despacio and their son. He had not been a man to feel much guilt about anything. He gave money to Sonya every time he was in Havana over a period of two years. After he stopped coming, he contributed nothing to her and Little Felix's welfare.

What could he do now to make up for this? Even if he located Sonya and Felix, Jr., he could not imagine that their response to him would be at all positive. He was an American gangster on his last legs—leg, actually—an enemy of the regime they had been living under and probably brainwashed by for the majority of their lives. Felix, Jr., of course, had never known any other way of life. The possibility did exist, Martucci realized, that she and the boy might have fled the island during the Mariel boatlift in 1981, or by some other means at another time. They could even be living in the United States right now.

A jet passed overhead, leaving in its wake a vapor trail a half-mile long that resembled a herd of elephants dispersing in several directions. Felix sipped his mojito, the first alcoholic drink he'd had in more than a year. He was reminded of the time Milwaukee Dave Indennizzare shot and killed a policeman in a whorehouse in the old section of Havana. The cop had gotten upset that Dave had taken his regular girl at the hour customarily reserved for him. There was an argument and the cop pulled his gun first. Dave had a drink in his hand, and he tossed it into the cop's face. The cop never fired a shot, but Dave got his piece out and nailed the cop. After the body had been removed from the premises, Dave asked for a fresh mojito to replace the one he'd wasted. When Lipsky heard the story he said from that time on Indennizzare should be called Mojito Dave.

Martucci hated thinking that his life was over, that there was no way to get it back, to have more time. He'd heard Walt Disney's head had been severed from its body and been preserved cryogenically in the hope that one day medical science would be able to reactivate his brain. Felix didn't want that—he just wanted to have a few more years as he was. It didn't look promising. Fuck complaining. Complaining was for the new generation. Those guys, all they knew how to do good was beef. Beef and betray each other. That's why this whole thing was over. Assimilation had done it. Blood meant nothing if it was thinned down too much.

Two more jet fighters flew over. Maybe on their way to or from Guantanamo, though the airspace directly over Havana, Felix thought, would have been severely restricted. Who knows what kinds of deals these politicians got.

A waiter came out onto the terrace and asked Felix if he wanted another drink. The waiter looked to be about forty years old.

"¿Cómo se llama?" Felix asked him.

"Benicio."

Martucci nodded and handed his almost empty glass to Benicio.

"*¿Porqué no?*"

The waiter placed the glass on a small tray and walked away. What if he'd said his name was Felix? What if he were the son of an old bad guy? What difference would it really make to anyone?

The sky clouded over. Felix reached down with his right hand and felt his cock through his trousers. He probably had prostate cancer, too, along with the heart condition. He'd read that eighty-five percent of all men eventually get cancer of the prostate, though most of them die of another ailment. Prostate cancer usually advanced slowly. He knew guys who'd had their prostates removed, surgery that left them impotent or incontinent or both. Better at this age just to let it go. At least he could still raise a hard-on now and again.

Benicio showed up with the mojito.

"Will there be anything else, sir," he asked in perfect English.

"Do you know a man in his early forties, looks a little like you, named Felix? Felix Despacio. His mother's name is Sonya."

"No, I don't believe so."

"Okay, then. Thanks."

Felix watched the waiter walk away, then he closed his eyes, resting the glass containing the rum concoction on his chest. He could hear the jets.

The Tunisian
Notebook

AUTHOR'S PREFACE

In April of 1914, the Swiss painters August Macke, Paul Klee and Louis René Moilliet embarked on a journey to North Africa to "capture the Mediterranean light." The trip lasted about two weeks, during which time they traveled from Marseilles to Tunis—St. Germain, to Sidi-bou-Said, to Carthage, to Hammamet, to Kairouan, and back to Tunis. Klee kept and later published his "Diary of Trip to Tunisia," which, according to Moilliet, Klee had endeavored to keep in a formal, literary style, resulting in the description of certain incidents being exaggerated or manufactured in keeping with Klee's vision of how events should properly have proceeded.

That same year, shortly after the outbreak of World War I, Macke was killed in action. It was not until 1979, sixty-five years after the Tunisian excursion, that this imaginary notebook, containing August Macke's own diary of the trip, was discovered. It provides an interesting contrast to Klee's perceptions, as well as being a valuable and illuminating document in its own right.

"Every people has its own manner of feeling, of telling
lies, of producing art.... One way of lying drives me to
the next one."

—AUGUST MACKE

"One always has to spoil a picture a little bit, in order
to finish it."

—EUGÈNE DELACROIX

Sunday, April 5, noon, Marseilles.

Arrived in Marseilles early this morning after travelling by ship
from Hilterfingen to Thun, then by train to Bern, where I
changed to the Southern Express. Throughout the journey I have
been thinking of Elisabeth, and wish now I had insisted she
accompany me, despite Louis and Paul. Never again. At least
there is the consolation of her having already seen Tunisia, but I
cannot help feeling it would be better were we together.

Perhaps my mood will change once I have met up with Louis
and Paul. They may be here now. I look forward to seeing
Moilliet—after all, it is because of an invitation from his friend
Jaeggi, the good doctor from Bern, now of Tunis, that this trip has
come about. With Klee it's different; we don't always get along,
not only personally but professionally. He doesn't like my poking
fun at "theory." Klee is already a fine artist but he's so premedi-
tated about everything. In deference to Louis I'll do my best not
to antagonize Klee, at least so long as he doesn't begin touting

Kandinsky to me! Will try to keep painterly discussion to a minimum, stick to the example of Cézanne and Delaunay.

Hot, tired, hungry—the usual condition. Downstairs for refreshment.

April 5, 11 P.M. Marseilles is a miracle of color! After eating I walked around the town, admiring the flowers, boats in the harbor, the clean, distinct whites, blues, yellows, greens and reds. A healthy breeze came up, which diminished my fatigue. Noticed a tall, striking woman with an unusual hairdo—amber curls piled high and spilling over her forehead—and followed her. She met some people outside of an arena where a bullfight was about to begin. As I'd never witnessed a bullfight I followed them in. The admission was cheap, a couple of francs.

The arrangement of shapes and contrasts in the crowd was spectacular, and far more interesting to watch than the spectacle itself. The bull was not killed but so poked and battered about that by the time the devils had done with the game it might have been kinder to murder the beast and spare it the misery of recovery, if indeed recovery were possible.

The bull began a thick, brown hue, with almost yellow horns, and became progressively darker during the ordeal. By the finish his hide was grayish-black, the horns sandy white. I forced myself to watch it all. I completely forgot the tall woman with the red-yellow curls. It became difficult to control myself, but somehow I managed to keep from being sick.

Afterwards walked along the quais and stopped at a sidewalk table on the Vieux Port. Sat over a vermouth until I felt sufficiently recovered, then ordered a big meal, which I was just finishing when Moilliet and Klee peeked over the hedge that surrounded the restaurant and spotted me.

I was glad to see them, and felt increasingly better as I described for them the woman with the odd hairdo and the bullfight. Louis remarked that Jaeggi had quite an eye for the ladies. Klee added that he thought it only appropriate that it should have been a woman to have led me to a scene of slaughter. Louis laughed and I reminded them that the bull, in France anyway, was allowed to survive. "You look healthy enough!" Klee said, and suggested that we go to the music hall, which we did.

Paul seemed especially to enjoy a comedy routine wherein a young man impersonated a Tyrolian girl, but neither Louis nor I were much taken by it. The performers seemed less than enthusiastic, their movements wooden and artificial, and so, too, the impression that remains, the colors somber and dim.

Walking back to the hotel I mentioned this to the others, pointing to a pair of violet birds perched on the lip of a bluish-gray rainspout. "Immortal moments meant to be captured."

But I was speaking more for the benefit of Klee than Moilliet. Louis understands. It was he who paid me the greatest compliment, last December, when we first met to discuss this venture. "Until I met you," Moilliet said, "I painted the way a man looks out the window."

Monday, April 6, 10 P.M., aboard the Carthage, the Mediterranean Sea.

We spent the morning exploring Marseilles. Klee was moved enough by the sights to consider staying on but Louis—"The Count," Klee calls him—regaled us with promises of greater treasures in the days ahead. Klee said the colors around Marseilles were "new." I disagreed politely—"They're only new to you because you've never seen them before." Louis got the joke but not Paul. Sometimes I think he is too serious to ever become a really great painter.

Boarded the Carthage at midday. A clean, freshly painted barque. A nice sail out of the harbor, but once in the Gulf of Lions each of us was forced, one by one, to take seasick pills. Klee's didn't work—he got them from Gabriele Münter—so I gave him some of mine and soon he was holding up all right.

Klee knows I don't think much of him sometimes—though I don't dislike him. He's jealous of my "success." What success? I asked Louis. Because Kohler likes my paintings and gives me something for them? Paul is dedicated, he'll have his day, perhaps more than one, and it will be bigger than either Moilliet's or mine, I fear, knowing the public taste. He is by far the toughest of us three.

My unreasonable prejudice against Klee begins with his pipe. He is a pipe-smoker, and I have, in my twenty-six years, yet to meet a pipe-smoker I didn't find to be a bore. Often a mean bore, the worst kind, the ones who insist on boring the hell out of you even after they've realized you're not in the least interested in what they're saying. Not that Klee is one of those—not yet anyway.

At dinner Louis and Paul ate like pigs, but I outdid them.

The seas are a steady six feet, the boat rolls, but not uncomfortably. Standing on deck tonight I could feel the sun waiting to come out.

Tuesday, April 7, 10:30 P.M., Tunis.

Klee is an early riser. By the time I came out on deck this morning he had breakfasted and begun sketching. "That's Sardinia," he told me, pointing toward the coastline.

I found Moilliet in the dining room. While we ate he told me how even as a child—they'd been schoolmates—Klee had been extraordinarily self-centered. Louis says Paul went forward and sat around with the third-class passengers for awhile. He likes to pretend he is one of them so that they will not react to him differently than they do to each other. This way, says Klee, he'll be able to capture their true expressions in his memory. He collects children's drawings, and saved many of those from his own childhood. Louis says Paul believes they hold the key to the future.

I don't mean to be going on all the time complaining about Klee and his attitudes. Perhaps there is something about him that I envy—his physical energy, or his confidence. Elisabeth is always joking about what she considers my laziness, but she only half-jokes, she must be serious or she wouldn't mention it so often. She remarks about it to guests. "Whatever will become of him when he grows old?" What she means by that I'm not certain. Perhaps I won't grow old.

It will be interesting to see what Klee accomplishes here. Actually I don't think he is half as adventuresome as I am, or even Moilliet. But he has an astonishing ability to relate objects and images historically. This evening at dinner he quoted Delacroix on North Africa—"every man I see is a Cato or a Brutus"—the Greco-Roman world incarnate. Paul is more well-read than I. But reading is more tiring than anything!

We spotted the African coast late in the day, at what seemed the pinnacle of the afternoon heat. It was white-green. Not until Sidi-bou-Said did we discern a land-shape, a hill covered with white dots—houses in regular up-and-down rows.

The boat navigated a narrow inlet which led to a long canal. It was white-hot and dead feeling, the water unmoving, though we could clearly see the Arabs along the shore in turbans and robes. We stood at the rail to try and catch a bit of wind, but the boat moved terribly slowly and the air was terrifically hot and sticky.

Klee commented ecstatically about the picturesqueness of the shoreline, and talked excitedly about the prospect of painting the Arab faces. I am not quite sure how to regard these remarks of his. It's as if he's just another philistine standing before an exquisite view, saying, "Beautiful, beautiful, beautiful," which reaction is the cheapest kind of traditional expression. But I know he's not. The manner of reacting varies not only with race but with personality. The Egyptians, the Chinese, the men of the Gothic age, Memling, Snyders, Cézanne, Mozart. The type of reaction varies as the human condition varies. Today it is impossible for an artist to work as a Renaissance or a Pompeiian artist worked. Most important is the conclusion: A Cézanne still life is as real as the wall on which it stands.

Dr. Jaeggi and his family—wife, daughter—met our boat and took us into Tunis, all of us squashed into their little yellow automobile. Jaeggi is a wonderful fellow, my age, very agreeable, just as Moilliet said he was. Louis likened him to Dr. Gachet, Van Gogh's doctor friend at Auvers. The Arabs call him "Father Jaeggi," and act like fawning children around him. He is an obstetrician. In Bern he was, at an extremely early age, a prominent surgeon. I meant to ask Louis—or Jaeggi himself—why he came to Tunisia. I must remember to do so tomorrow. His wife and daughter are lovely—the girl has a dancing face.

Jaeggi took us to his house in St. Germain—he keeps an office in Tunis, at No. 2 Bab-el-Allouch, his card says—where we rested and recovered from the intense heat under large fans, and then had a superb meal prepared by Frau Jaeggi and the servant Ahmed, a lithe, chocolate fellow with a brilliant smile. Jaeggi says that he, Ahmed, is a genuine artist, a good one.

After dinner Jaeggi drove me into the city to the Hôtel de France—the others are staying at the house—and saw that I was properly settled before leaving me. On the way in the car he told me how pleased he was that we—through Moilliet—had accepted his invitation, and that I, too, was welcome to stay in St. Germain. I thanked him and explained that, unlike Louis and Paul, I had a patron, and could afford the luxury of a hotel, adding that it would be less work for Ahmed and Frau Jaeggi. He said I was welcome to change my mind at any time.

The night air is sweet and warm. Tunisia is already a pleasant surprise.

Wednesday, April 8, midnight, St. Germain.
Louis and Paul arrived early this morning with Jaeggi, in his car. I hadn't had breakfast as yet so they accompanied me to a café near the marketplace. While I ate they shopped at nearby stalls— the souks.

Jaeggi sat and had a coffee, telling me he's never bothered to get a license, here or in Bern. A driver's license, that is. He says he's never been reprimanded for not having one, not even when stopped by the police for some reason. They see his identification as a doctor and make their apologies for having delayed him. Why bother with a driver's permit when a medical certificate will do? Jaeggi's an extraordinary man.

Tunisia is a real world, he told me, not an artificial one like Europe, with its parks and gardens. "Paint what you see," he said, "it's enough." If by "real" he means no derby hats or Paris styles he is correct.

Moilliet came over to tell us of a funeral procession. We could hear the wailing and moaning and then a cart drawn by six scrawny mules clattered slowly past the café, a blue and gold coffin strapped onto it. Louis followed after it, fascinated. Ever since old Gobat's death he has been exceedingly passionate about funerals.

The rest of us went along and watched as the burial was accomplished in a little field just beyond the market. Klee kept his smile fixed just so. He thinks Louis is a bit of a fool and that I am too set in my ways. He's right, but so what?

After a short tour courtesy of Dr. Jaeggi, he went to his office and I decided to explore the native quarter on my own, enlisting the aid of a policeman who observed me buying charcoals and paints. I asked him if he could guide me to the more interesting spots, the whorehouses, drug dens, etc. Who should know better than a police officer where to go?

For not very much money he agreed to show me around and, presumably, abandoned his official duties for the remainder of the afternoon. Klee refused to go along, though I hadn't asked him to come with me. He seemed upset and wanted to make his disapproval known, but I didn't pay him much attention. He and Moilliet went off to explore some mosques.

Abdoul, the policeman, earned his francs, showing me, in fact, more than I could absorb in an afternoon. I made dozens of sketches, several of the prostitutes in a house on Rue Rouge, lounging on divans in negligees, their necks strung with pearls, smoking and joking with one another. They were very familiar with Abdoul, as I'd guessed they'd be. I gave them each a sketch of themselves and they seemed quite taken by them. I promised to return soon, without my drawing materials, and they all laughed. To my surprise they appeared to be very bright girls.

There is so much here to attract the eye! Ornate, arched gates, bazaars, the market, terraces with awnings, tents, domes of mosques, mules, camels, and these beautiful, brown-skinned people.

In the evening drove with Jaeggi out to St. Germain for dinner. He would like Klee and me to paint the interior of his studio. We agreed to do so. I am staying the night, much to the apparent displeasure of the housemaid, a heavy, sweaty girl from Aargau, who did a poor job of preparing my bed. I mentioned this to Louis a few moments ago in the hall. "There's one thing the Aargau girl does know how to do," he said, "to draw a bath! That she does perfectly."

Thursday, April 9, 11 P.M., Tunis.
After breakfast Jaeggi drove Klee and me into town, left us at the hotel, and continued on to his surgery. Paul insisted that I accompany him to the harbor to paint. I made a number of small paintings, but was so bothered by the coal dust in my eyes and in the watercolors that I was forced to stop. Klee worked on despite the conditions, and in the face of taunts by crew members of a French torpedo boat tied up nearby, who cursed us in broken German.

I ate lunch alone in the same café as yesterday and then wandered on my own until I found the tomb of a Marabu, a Moslem saint. My policeman told me yesterday they were everywhere because Arab saints were always buried on the spot where they died. There are many in Tunis and, apparently, in and around Sidi-bou-Said. I did a painting of the entranceway, without interference from dust, sailors, or fellow artists!

Met Louis and Paul for supper and afterwards went with them to a concert Arabe. They are real tourists, as obvious as though they wore large red badges emblazoned with the word itself. Moilliet, because of his naiveté, is the easier to accept, but Klee looks down on the natives. His condescending conversation is insufferable. There is nothing barbaric about belly dancing. The women and their glistening skin adorned with multifarious decorations form a symmetry that is a kinetic delight. Tunisia is not a prudish country. Paul pretends he is undisturbed by this kind of performance; Louis exults. I am someplace in between.

Friday, April 10, 9 P.M., Tunis.

Made sixty sketches today! A truly inspired one for me. I share Klee's respect for the images of childhood and children's works of art. To produce true art one must experience a rebirth, as does nature with each fresh season. One must tap the flow of nature in order to be able to create art in a musical, Mozartian manner.

The day was filled with such a lively, pristine, childlike light that I had no thoughts of eating. Upon arising I dressed quickly, gathered up my paints and pencils and the paper I brought from Switzerland, and hurried out into the street without bothering about washing. By noon I'd done two dozen drawings and felt fresh as ever.

I stopped in the market to buy some fruit but instead fell into conversation with an Italian photographer who showed me a portfolio of amazing pictures. I bought fifteen of them, portraits of women in many imaginative positions, which I showed around the dinner table this evening at the house of Captain Lecoq. Lecoq is a friend of Jaeggi's, a French officer who is quite popular with the Arabs since he has taken their side against the government in Paris. He says after ten years in Tunis he feels more like an Arab than a Frenchman—Lecoq is not an ordinary official, he is quite outgoing. He practically licked the photographs and made some appropriately wicked remarks concerning the poses. After dinner he asked me if I'd yet visited any of the houses in the Quarter. When I told him I had, but only to make drawings, he looked at me strangely. Then I told him I was in the company of a policeman. Lecoq laughed and said the policeman must have been very amused. "The behavior of foreigners never ceases to amaze."

Saturday, April 11, 11:45 P.M., St. Germain.
Spent a couple of hours in and around the market this morning looking for something to bring Elisabeth. I bought her several uniquely detailed pieces of embroidery and an amber necklace—

a Mohammedan rosary—with a stone seal from Achat inlaid with mysterious signs, and a pair of yellow slippers for myself. Wrote her a letter, the first since our arrival, and a short one at that. There are too many things to do and see to spend one's time writing letters.

Jaeggi called for me at the hotel about three, and we drove out to St. Germain. Sat on the terrace drinking wine and talking with Jaeggi—a pleasant afternoon. He is actually a bit younger than I, a renowned surgeon, and yet he insists on calling me the "accomplished" one.

Jaeggi told me the story of Lecoq's infatuation with a thirteen-year-old Arab girl. Apparently she came to him every day for six months until her father found out about it. Because Lecoq gave the girl money now and then the mother begged her husband not to do anything—and of course as an officer of the French garrison Lecoq commands substantial political power. But the father went berserk and attacked Lecoq with a knife. Lecoq shot him dead. Immediately thereafter he was given a holiday leave, which he spent in France. He returned to Tunis a month later, by which time both the girl and her mother had disappeared.

Klee came in from working on the beach. Louis was sketching the sunset from the balcony. Jaeggi suggested we decorate Easter eggs for the holiday tomorrow, which we did. Ahmed brought them in and helped make the designs. His eggs were far more intricately fashioned than any of ours, supporting Jaeggi's judgment of his talent.

After another generous and well-prepared dinner, Klee and I set to the dining room wall. Klee contented himself with a few doodles in the corners, while I marked out a six-foot square in the middle in which I depicted a market scene—a small black donkey laden with baskets of oranges, flanked by two redtarbooshed Arab drivers. Jaeggi seemed more than a little pleased with our work.

Moilliet opened a bottle of brandy for the occasion, and insisted we finish it before retiring. Curiously, I don't feel at all drunk, only fatigued from the constant heat, which I doubt I could ever get used to.

Easter Sunday, April 12, 4 P.M., Tunis.
A poor day for me. Holidays are not the time to be away from home. I fear I miss Elisabeth and my sons too much. Tried to rouse myself from the doldrums at Jaeggi's, drew a picture of his daughter and gave it to her—her parents will frame it and hang it in her room—but was unsuccessful. I dare not write home while I am in this condition.

I joined feebly in the hunt for the eggs. Klee was upset that the colors came off on our fingers, but nobody else seemed to mind.

Jaeggi drove me into Tunis and deposited me at the hotel so that I could rest without being disturbed before our journey tomorrow to Hammamet. There is a measurable amount of moisture in the air.

Tuesday, April 14, 10:30 P.M., Hammamet.

Slept all day yesterday, therefore no entry in the notebook. Had to postpone our travel plans until today. It must have been a slight case of influenza that brought on my melancholia.

Louis and Paul were in good spirits throughout the trip. They seemed to have been inspired by the dawn departure. The ancient locomotive wound slowly through stretches of desert broken occasionally by pathetic patches of forest. Moilliet (with his bottle of brandy—he is not without one these days) and Klee were enraptured by the—to me—sparse scenery.

Outside Hammamet station we spent half an hour watching a camel, instructed by a veiled young woman, draw water from a well by walking back and forth pulling a rope attached to a bucket. A time-tested method. Klee would have remained there forever had Louis and I not threatened to go on without him. Paul worships the primitive.

Spent the day with watercolors in the main cemetery. Unlike in Tunis, here we are free to explore them. Fabulous cactuses tower over us. From a distance they resemble the great dusty buildings of an abandoned city. I set up my things on a small hill from which I could observe the crooked coastline and benefit from a gentle but steady breeze.

Found lodging in a rooming house run by a tough old dame who claims she's French, from Nice, but she's an Arab. Smokes black tobacco. Her fingers are deeply stained. For dinner she offered us cow liver, so we went to a café instead. The food there was not very appealing either, but we had a light meal while being "entertained" by a blind nasal singer accompanied by a young boy on a drum.

After dinner we followed the noise of a band to a little street fair, where we watched a fakir let a cobra bite him on the nose and another devour live scorpions.

Louis and I finished off his brandy, the melancholic's companion.

Wednesday, April 15, just past midnight, Kairouan.
Quite a trip today. This morning trekked to Bir-bou-rekba from Hammamet, earning curious stares from robed Arabs along the road. Passersby spat greetings to us, nodding and smiling. Three European gentlemen on foot, wearing suits and straw hats, packing gear on their backs—surely as ridiculous a sight as they've ever seen. It was Louis who insisted we walk, to "gain the feel" of the province.

It was actually quite a short distance, perhaps two kilometers, to the Bir-bou-rekba station, where we boarded a train to Kalaa-srira. There we stopped for lunch at a dusty café run by a black Arab madman in a torn red djilaba. Dozens of wild chickens ran amongst the tables searching for drops of food in the dust. Moilliet was undisturbed by the situation—he smiled and sipped his brandy. Klee and I attempted to order, but the proprietor chased insanely around after the chickens, shouting threats on the life of his neighbor, to whom the fowl belonged.

Soon all of the customers were laughing and taunting the restaurant owner. I took the remnants of a meal from an abandoned nearby table and scattered the bits on the ground, causing a crazed clucking, screeching, dust-swirling stampede. The chickens were now hopping onto the tables and chairs and the poor proprietor was beside himself.

He yelled at me to stop encouraging the beasts, to please not throw them breadcrumbs. I responded indignantly—"But sir, I wouldn't dare to feed them breadcrumbs, I'm giving them cheese!"

After that the unfortunate man gave up. All we managed to pry from his kitchen was some weak coffee, for which we reluctantly paid three francs. At that moment our train entered the station and we embarked for Kairouan. After a brief stopover in Acouda, which from the train appeared as a raging storm of flies and dust, we arrived in Kairouan in mid-afternoon.

Found a French hotel in the center of town—the Marseilles—ate, drank, slept until evening. No work. Tonight attended a marriage feast—the daughter of the hotel proprietor and a local, apparently well-to-do businessman. A magnificent outdoor banquet: roasted lamb, chicken, dozens of unfamiliar delicacies. We ate and drank everything that was offered. Klee was ecstatic—for the first time on the trip he looked completely relaxed.

Thursday, April 16, 8 P.M., Tunis.
The Tunisian sky in the moment before dawn is mysteriously affecting. Watching it brighten my feeling of personal insignifi-

cance increased. Reds, blues, yellows folded over and under one another, orange clouds, merged and parted in a living collage. Finally, light, pure light, orchestrated by camel groans and dispersing shadows, a gray-pink cat without a tail stretching and rolling over in the dust.

Made a series of paintings in the morning, a herdsman in red fez and brown robe, two heavily draped women on the road to the city, date trees, domed roofs, a leopard-faced boy in the town square. This afternoon we hired a guide, who showed us through the local mosques. He expressed interest in learning German, so I taught him the words for white, black, shit, piss, fuck, eat and how much. A sufficient vocabulary in any language.

Arrived back in Tunis at dusk. Louis joined the Jaeggis at Lecoq's, Klee went off to spend some time alone, and I took a long bath at the hotel, after which I found Paul at the Chianti restaurant and stuffed myself with pasta al pesto. Paul is planning to leave for home on Sunday. He thinks Louis intends to stay on for a few days past that. I would like to stay longer also, and will speak to Moilliet about it tomorrow.

Friday, April 17, 11 P.M., Tunis.
Sketched until noon in the marketplace. Thus far I've made more than thirty watercolors and dozens of drawings. Wrote a short letter—only the second since I've been gone—to Elisabeth, telling her I will be bringing some colossal things back with me. I must travel more often to exotic places! I seem able to see

everything so clearly, to understand the people by an expression, a tilt of the head. Because of my unfamiliarity with them, things become more distinct.

We took an afternoon trip back to Kalaa-srira to see a mosque Klee heard about last night. Had tea and bread at the madman's café—no chickens! He must have poisoned them all. The mosque was less than spectacular, a rather ordinary facade and whitewashed interior, and we were there at the wrong hour—and apparently the wrong season—to witness the angles of light that distinguished it. Moilliet and I were bored, the waste of an afternoon.

On the way to Tunis we wrestled in the train compartment— Louis and I, that is. Klee is outraged by this kind of behavior. He says the Arabs will think less of us if we act improperly, i.e., "un-European." Any manner of physical spontaneity disgusts him. I can't take too much of Klee—and he considers me facile, I know. It's just as well we don't have much time left together.

Had dinner alone in a café near the hotel, and read the first European newspaper I've seen since coming to Tunisia. My interest in that world has drastically diminished. If it weren't for the unsanitary conditions, I think I should like to stay on in North Africa indefinitely.

Saturday, April 18, after midnight, Tunis.
Just returned from a marvelous evening at Jaeggi's, where we all got drunk and made passes at everyone's wives. Louis passed

around my famous Italian photographs, which were universally admired—especially by the ladies—and that got everything started. Jaeggi's other dinner guests—there were sixteen in all—had been invited, in view of our impending departure, for a farewell celebration.

I'm afraid I'm too drunk to write very much or very well. When one officer's wife asked me where I'd bought the pictures—which she called "French cards"—I told her to please take for herself her favorite one. I thought my offer would be humorously rejected, but the lady surprised me by choosing one of my own favorites and depositing it in her purse!

The rest of the day was rather dull; I remember very little other than that it rained steadily for the first time, putting the natives in a good mood.

Sunday, April 19, 6 P.M., Tunis.
Back from seeing Klee off, third class on a rusty tub. He pretends to be happy when he's miserable, a compulsion with which I have no sympathy. The day has been taken up with farewell conversations and the gathering together of belongings. Moilliet and I will leave tomorrow for Thun via Palermo and Rome. The Jaeggis are wonderful people. They have been glad to see us, and now they're glad to see us go, which is how it should be.

Time to eat, and afterwards, perhaps a stroll in the light rain.

The Unspoken
(*Il Nondetto*)

Translated from the Italian of an anonymous author

1

I begin like any other man, without a plan. I am staying in a seaside resort, one of many, in no particular country; perhaps somewhere on the Ionian Sea. Yes, I recall the insignificant waves,
waves hardly to be disturbed by. There is a beach, of course,
though I avoid sand; it reminds me so painfully of the deserts of
my childhood. The many flowers are in bloom but I can never
remember the names of flowers or plants other than bouganvil-
lea, which grew everywhere around the town. For these flowers
to thrive the weather must remain hot for several months, which
it does. It is very hot every day, each day of my residence.

I was born without a mouth. Can you believe this? I am forty-
eight years old, I have been living for almost a half-century with
this condition, an extraordinary circumstance, and yet I find this
situation incomprehensible. It is also ridiculous not to have a
mouth. Think of it—of course, you already have—to be unable

to talk or eat in a conventional manner. One never grows used to this handicap. At least, I have not.

The absence of a mouth—my mouth, the one intended for me (I have always believed that God intended to give me a mouth; this belief is unshakeable)—has no bearing on this story. An adventure has a life of its own, and my life, 'the life of a natural freak, is irrelevant here (other than as a terrible detail that I implore you to ignore). I do not even know or understand why I mention it. (Perhaps being without a mouth, the idea of this crime, obsesses me and will lead to an unfortunate circumstance. We shall see.)

Did I mention that I am alone in this seaside village? I am isolated if not alone in the strictest sense of the term. By definition a person has no choice in the matter. (Or have you, the reader, chosen not to question whatever myth with which you have been informed? It doesn't matter, it really doesn't. Believe me.) There are no birds on the island. (Is it an island? I can't remember.) This is an amazing fact, a stupendous argument against logic. Consider you are at the seaside and are expecting, as you should, to see birds, a flock of them, a single frigate or tern or gull, and after two days you experience the terrible realization that no birds exist. This is what happened to me. (I would have asked someone, a fellow guest at the hotel where I am staying, but of course, as you now know and cannot forget— I won't let you, you can be certain—I had no mouth with which to do so. Being supremely unlike any other person will have its disadvantages, as well as advantages an ordinary individual could not begin to imagine.)

The absence of birds notwithstanding, I decided to stay. I will not keep you in suspense any longer—Why should I, a man without a motive, or a mouth?—the reason I fled the city (a large one, named R.), exchanged it like a soiled glove (I am very fond of gloves) for the featherless seaside resort town (I will call it T.), had to do with a woman. She rejected me, after several years of friendship. I must bite my tongue (figuratively speaking—but then, neither am I able to speak) as I write that. If you have read this far in my narrative, you are not readily or easily fooled. Forgive me for not being entirely honest at the outset. (I feel more ridiculous asking for forgiveness than I do upon entering a public place where nobody knows me and they stare at the area of my face below the nose where a mouth, any kind of mouth— even a narrow one, with thin lips—should, by all God intended, be.) F. and I had been lovers for four years. This fact is inescapable. I must admit that it gives me pleasure (a pleasure of sorts, I suppose) to say this. Is it incomprehensible to you that a woman as beautiful (I believe she is beautiful) and intelligent (this, too, though remember I am easily fooled) as F. should have accepted for her lover a man without a certain feature? Of course, had she not been an extraordinary person to begin with I could not have loved her. I still love her. Though we are no longer together, it does not mean that my powerful feeling for F. has ceased to exist. I am essentially an honest man.

2

I had, as I say, no plan when I arrived at T. I had never even considered going to T., had never heard of the place before my last-minute departure. No, that is not entirely true; I had heard of T. When I was a boy, our housekeeper, M., used to mention the place now and again. I believe she had some relatives there that she would visit on occasion. M. had beautiful feet. I first saw them when I crawled around the house, before I could walk, and M. would do her chores barefoot. Her feet were extraordinarily long and slender, like ferrets. It was painful for me when my parents fired M. for stealing. I was then seven years old. I thought that M. would return sometime, but she never did. Luckily, I have no problem conjuring up images of her perfect heels, delicate arches and exquisite toes. F.'s feet are much smaller, her toes bent in various directions, tortured worms. I cannot consider them in the same category with those of M., the angelic housekeeper of my youth.

The subject, the suggestion of T., of my going there, presented itself late one night as I was riding in a taxi. It had been raining all that day and into the evening. The streets and buildings of the city in which I live were blackened by water. The entire city resembled a discarded tire floating in the sea. For a moment the downpour abated, and when the taxi froze suddenly at a stoplight I could see through the glass a poster hanging in a shop window advertising T. Just as suddenly, the taxi sped forward again, forcing the issue; it would be necessary for me to investigate the possibility of T.

It is important for me to accept what I now recognize as F.'s morbid self-image in regard to my anatomical anomaly. (How many ways, after all, is it possible to say "without a mouth"?) I believe absolutely that she enjoyed becoming involved with my predicament. Whether this intrigue included a particular sexual component on her part I (naturally) cannot say. F.'s fondness for brushing her lips along that area of my face below my nose and above my chin I did not attribute to any bizarre fascination. After all, other than with their genitals, this is the most natural place for lovers to combine. Sympathy for her arose in me, however, when (though she never spoke of it) I realized how often she yearned to be kissed. Regardless of our repeated coupling, a sense of something missing progressively became an overwhelming factor in our relationship.

A surgical remedy was out of the question. As a child, I was subjected to numerous medical examinations. Due to an unusual (What is not unusual in this case?) configuration of blood vessels in what should have been my orthodontal region, the specialists deemed invasive measures too precarious for purposes of plastic reconstruction.

The first question, of course, is always: How do you eat? In ancient times, I would have been slaughtered at birth. At first sight, upon expulsion from my mother's womb, the hideous creature— I—would certainly have had the briefest of sojourns on this earth. It is believed that a baby does not exercise its vision for two or three weeks, in which case never would I have been able to experience sight, my greatest pleasure. The question of sustenance never would have been raised. As it is, in this most medically aggressive age intravenous feeding has become almost de rigeur. I possess all relevant bodily functions; several times a day, at my convenience, I am sustained via injection. At the age of three, desiring to emulate my playmates, I attempted to ingest regular food—carrots, I believe—through my nostrils. I succeeded only in very nearly asphyxiating myself. This terrible lesson served me well. I knew then, barely beyond infancy, that I controlled death. Subsequently, of course, I learned of the infinite ways in which death controlled me, and that I was an amateur in this department, a novice for whom sophistication would remain a hopeless fantasy.

3

If nobody had a mouth then who would inhabit the lie? How would it be verbalized? How could any condition beyond death go unrecognized? F., being beyond life—my life, for now (or forever)—is also beyond death. She has no choice but to exist forever (for now) at variance with the universe as I perceive it. Perception is not properly open to competition. Opinions are replaced repeatedly and with increasing facility. Nothing can prevent this.

It was not F.'s way to directly reprimand me; never would she act so overtly. Unpleasant circumstances provoked her to laughter, a response which she herself found baffling. This enigmatic mirth, I informed F., was a not uncommon nervous reaction; an obviously involuntary seizure belieing no especial significance.

F., however, believed her behavior at such moments to be most unseemly; nothing I could say could disabuse her of this opinion.

4

F., then, for the sake of this story, which is, of course, not a story. (I never really intended it to be.) If I say she is tall and dark, or fragile, just that, it conveys so very little. There is a darkness in her that she struggles to avoid; it eats at her like a rash on the inside of her skin. The way she moves expresses inexorable distress. Often her movements are those of a lizard on a terrace in the hot sun. She skitters, stops, jerks her head, flaps her eyelids (Do lizards have eyelids? If not, why not?), runs on, light evaporating the colors on her spine: green and blue become gray. F. is serious as she pretends to gaiety. It frightens and—I must confess—delights me. Her vulnerability shrieks at the sky.

I adore F. and do not blame her for her defection. A predicament such as mine is not nullifying, not in any sense expressive of finality. At least it does not impress me in this way. F., on the other hand, has imposed upon herself a philosophy so restrictive in its parameters that there is virtually no opportunity for her to entirely relax. I do not refer particularly to her impatience with me. How would it be possible for a person—any person with even adequate intelligence and perceptivity—not to be occasionally intolerant?

It is quite common for people to convulse in the presence of a freak. Even F. has become overwhelmed at the sight of me, despite our long association. She will begin to think of me as being entirely normal in appearance, then suddenly turn to speak to me and be shocked at what she sees. The fear in her eyes when this occurs is unmistakable. Her heart palpitates, her throat and mouth dry up, she stutters when she attempts to regain her faculties. I must remain calm at such moments, endure these seizures of naivete without a flinch of self-hatred.

I do not loathe myself, after all; it is everyone else whom I loathe. Others have not the complete privilege of seeing how disgustingly weak they are. Confrontation connotes nausea, and this incautious behavior precludes the possibilities of seriousness.

Only You

There was a short article in the San Francisco newspaper about how various building materials used in construction of housing designed for and allocated to low-income, disabled people and their families were causing allergic reactions in the residents. One of the occupants quoted to this effect was a middle-aged woman named Honey Adams who complained that she had a pre-existing condition which made her particularly sensitive to some of the chemicals used in the treatment of flooring and wall-board in her housing unit. She added that her nineteen-year-old daughter, who lived with her, suffered from the same malady. The article stated that Honey Adams had waited two years to move into her rent-controlled apartment. "I have no alternative now," she said. "I gave up the place I had before in order to move in here, only to find out the environment is toxic."

The name Honey Adams meant something to me: Thirty years before, when I was a student at the University of Texas, I had had a girlfriend by that name. I had not been back there in almost that long and I'd lived in San Francisco for more than twenty years. I wondered if this could possibly be the same

Honey Adams, whom I had not seen or been in contact with since my one and only year in Texas.

That evening on one of the local television news programs there was a feature on the problem of disabled persons' housing being potentially toxic. I watched as a woman identified as Honey Adams, whose profession was given as "fiction writer," was interviewed. This woman was grossly overweight, her face was puffy, she wore glasses and her gray hair cut short. She used a cane when she walked. It was a different Honey Adams than the one I had known. The camera panned around the apartment and there, pointing to something on the floor, was the Honey Adams I remembered. This girl had gorgeous long, wavy, red-gold hair; she was slender with a beautiful figure and face. Her big green eyes stared into the camera for a moment and my heart jumped: She was Honey's daughter.

I turned off the television and thought about Honey at Texas. She was three years older than I, a senior at the university; I was a freshman. We were both enrolled in a class called Narration, a kind of beginner's course in creative writing. I wasn't the only one to notice Honey Adams, of course. There were thirteen or fourteen students in the class and each of the six boys had difficulty keeping their eyes off of her. She was a genuine knock-out.

Honey and I ran into each other one night at a party and talked for a while; then, even though we had both arrived with dates, we took a walk during which we paused to kiss several times, stopping just short of doing anything more serious. That didn't happen until the next night, after which we kept steady company for several weeks.

Honey was a "townie." She lived with her mother, who was completely deaf. She spoke, however, very softly; because of this and the way she slurred her words, I seldom understood what she said. Honey, though, had no problems understanding her. They had lived in a small town in Wisconsin, where Honey was born, until Honey's father died. She was thirteen at the time. After his death Honey's mother moved them to Austin, Texas, where she was originally from and still had family.

A year or so before I met her, Honey had spent a summer with cousins in Los Angeles. She couldn't wait, she told me, to go back to California. That's where she wanted to live. Honey intended to write novels and maybe even movies, she said. She admitted that she didn't know yet if she had any real talent but that would come with time. After reading a few of my stories and poems, Honey delightedly told me that she was sure I would be a successful writer, that I had something special, my own way of saying things. She hoped one day she would be able to believe the same about her own work.

Everything seemed wonderful to me in that moment. I was certain that I was in love with Honey and that she loved me. I began to think about going with her to California after she graduated the following June. Then one afternoon she came to the room that I rented in an old wooden house on a hill and told me she would not be able to date me any more. She was three years older and she was going away soon; we would have to separate and she didn't want either of us to bear the burden of trying to maintain a serious relationship while we were so young. We needed to explore the world, she said, and our lives as writers without encumbrances.

I asked Honey if she loved me and she said she thought so but that it didn't matter. She had decided not to see me in this intimate way again. If we continued as we were it would be much more difficult to separate. I told her we could go to California together, that wasn't a problem. I had decided to leave school anyway, I didn't want to be a student. I needed to travel and just write.

Honey smiled and kissed me. "You will write," she said. "You'll be a great writer and travel everywhere. I hope I will, too, but it'll be better for us to be apart right now, I know it."

I didn't want to argue with her; her mind was made up, so I let it go. After that, whenever we ran into each other on the campus or in town, I just said hello and moved on. Until I saw her on the television news thirty years later, other than as a memory Honey Adams had been lost to me.

After the program I thought about calling Honey. Her telephone number was probably listed; if not, I could have contacted her through the television station. In the end, I decided against it. She was no longer the Honey I remembered from Texas—certainly I was no longer the same, either—and although her reasons might be different now, I suspected that she still did not want to see me.

Vendetta

Gino told me this story about an old man in his neighborhood in the Bronx named Mario who was connected. This was in 1969. Apparently Mario's crew had an ongoing beef with a rival gang and one morning Mario opened his front door and found a dead body on his doorstep. Mario didn't touch it. He closed the door to his house, stepped carefully over the stiff and went to his office, like he did every day of the week.

Later, the cops quizzed him. Why didn't he notify them about the body?

"What body?" he asked.

"The corpse was dumped in your doorway before dawn. You couldn't miss it."

"I didn't see no corpse."

"Come off it, Mario. It was one of your soldiers, Carmello Cerrone."

"What soldiers? I ain't in the army."

"A woman walking to work saw the body, called us."

"A woman from the neighborhood?"

"No, a cleaning lady. You can't get away with this."

Mario laughed. "I ain't tryna geddaway with nothin'.

I didn't see what I didn't see. And you know what else? They didn't land on no moon."

"What're you talkin' about?"

"There weren't no men on the moon. That was Arizona! Tryna fool people like that, they should be arrested."

"Who should be arrested, Mario?"

"The government. Put a stooge in a divin' costume out inna desert, tell the world they got a man onna moon. It's criminal."

"Are you saying you didn't see the dead body of Carmello Cerrone on the front steps of your house this morning?"

"You guys got bad memories. I already told you. Just like I'm tellin' you it was in Arizona they landed, not the freakin' moon."

"That was the end of the investigation," said Gino. "The cops couldn't shake a thing out of him. Mario wasn't fooling about the astronauts, though. He was convinced the moonwalk was a bad con. The old man couldn't believe everyone didn't see it."

New Mysteries
of Paris

I was recently told a story that was so stupid, so melancholy, and so moving: a man comes into a hotel one day and asks to rent a room. He is shown up to number 35. As he comes down a few minutes later and leaves the key at the desk, he says: "Excuse me, I have no memory at all. If you please, each time I come in, I'll tell you my name: Monsieur Delouit. And each time you'll tell me the number of my room."—"Very well, Monsieur." Soon afterwards he returns, and as he passes the desk says: "Monsieur Delouit."—"Number 35, Monsieur."—"Thank you." A minute later, a man extraordinarily upset, his clothes covered with mud, bleeding, his face almost not a face at all, appears at the desk: "Monsieur Delouit."—"What do you mean, Monsieur Delouit? Don't try to put one over on us! Monsieur Delouit has just gone upstairs!"—"I'm sorry, it's me.... I've just fallen out of the window. What's the number of my room, please?"

ANDRÉ BRETON

Nadja was taken to a madhouse in 1928. Someplace in the French countryside where ordinary people, those fortunate enough to have escaped scrutiny, who have avoided so far in their lives being similarly judged and sentenced and dismissed from the greater society, will not be reminded of their own failings by the screams of the outcast.

It is reasonable to suppose that by that time there could not be much difference for Nadja between the inside of a sanitarium and the outside—but Nadja was here, she left something of herself. Certainly she's dead by now, buried in a field behind an insane asylum, cats screwing on her grave.

The day she threatened to jump from the window of her room in the Hotel Sphinx on the Boulevard Magenta I should have known she was not a fake. Who can tell the genuine mad from the fake? Nadja could. She was always pointing them out to me. In a café she'd whisper, "Look at her. Biting her nails. Pretending to be waiting for someone. She's a fake. Her lovers disappear." "But how can you tell?" I'd ask. "Look at my eyes," Nadja would say. "Can you see the way they are lit from behind? I'm dangerous. To be avoided."

Who was Nadja? What was the significance of Nadja in my life? Why does she return, a constant, though I've not seen nor heard of or from her in fifty years?

I saw a woman in a marketplace in a Mexican city, Mérida, perhaps, in the Yucatán, twenty years ago or so. She resembled

Nadja, or what she might have looked like, according to my idea of Nadja had she still been alive, let alone an inhabitant of a jungle town in Mexico. I followed her as she moved from stand to stand, inspecting the fruits, dresses, beads, kitchen knives, crucifixes. Was this a woman or a phantom? Her gray hair was worn long and thick and fell across her face so that her features were indistinct, shadowed. Nadja had been blonde, with the short, curled haircut of the day, a brief nose, sharp black hawk's eyes, a long mouth with slender lips, purple, that grinned in one corner only. This hag in the marketplace was fat, toothless, I would say, judging by the line of her jaw, dark-skinned. Nadja had been white as the full moon of February over Venice, almost emaciated, seldom ate, with a full mouth of teeth, crooked but strong. She was capable of cracking open with ease in one swift bite a stalk of Haitian sugarcane.

How could I imagine this hideous, crumbling jungle creature to be Nadja? Some feeling made me follow until, crossing a busy street, I lost sight of her. I panicked and looked around wildly. She was gone and I was forced to suppress a great scream of pain. Unused to this severe sort of anxiety, I battled to control my emotions, there in the midst of a crowd of Indians.

It was what Nadja had meant when she stuck her tongue into my ear as we rode in a cab along the Boulevard Raspail. As quickly as she'd done it she withdrew to the opposite corner of the seat and said, staring blankly ahead, "To me nothing is more terrifying than the curse of self-fulfillment."

What did Nadja do before we met? I asked her many times and mostly she would avoid answering by laughing and kissing me, adjusting my tie or brushing my lapels. She did tell me she was born in Belgium, near Ghent, and that her father raised flowers. She went to the local school, in a convent, and moved to Paris when she was seventeen. She met a man, unidentified, got married, gave birth to a daughter, who promptly died of pneumonia. Those were facts, according to Nadja. The man was gone soon after the daughter.

Other than that there was little Nadja would admit. None of it was important, she said. "Not to you!" She instructed me to invent her story, it was all the same, unrelated to today. "Who is the hero of a film that has at its center a peacock flying through and landing in the snow?" Nadja asks, licking my chin as if she were here.

I must recall exactly how and why I became involved with Nadja. I was walking along the Rue Vaugirard, preparing to turn into the Luxembourg, when I saw a woman standing in front of a butcher's shop desperately examining the contents of her purse. I say desperately because there were lines of great consternation on her face, as if she had misplaced and was frantically searching for the ticket that would allow her to claim a side of beef she'd pawned or left to be laundered. The weather was foul, it was early November and it was raining. The air was ugly, full of woodsmoke and water, black, brown and gray. The woman, who was Nadja, was a disconcerting sight, her hair matted, stockings torn, coat soaked. I approached her immediately and asked if I might be of service.

"This is an evil afternoon," she said. She looked at me. "Can you buy me a drink? There are ravens everywhere now. Even in the shops, in the road. The government is full of them, as you no doubt are already aware. What would a government be without its ravens?" She stared at me with horrible yellow eyes. There was no possibility of refusal. "Of course," I said, and Nadja smiled, a sweet, genuine smile, and gently took my arm.

Nadja had a harelip. Have I mentioned that? Or had been born with a harelip. She'd had it fixed, but that was the reason for her lopsided grin that added so inexplicably to Nadja's desirability.

She disliked being thought of as foolish, though she often sought to contribute to the common good by committing foolish acts, such as disrobing in the Louvre in front of the Mona Lisa. For that "act of valor," as Nadja referred to it, she spent several days in jail, not having the money to pay the fine for being a public nuisance.

Following the incident at the Louvre, Nadja made a similar gesture of liberation on the Avenue d'Iena near the German Club. The Germans, she claimed, would not have her arrested; instead, Nadja said, they would pretend to ignore her. Then came the affair at Trocadero where Nadja disrobed and poured a bucket of red paint over her head. Neither time was she detained. The Mona Lisa episode had made her famous for the moment and her exploits of this order were no longer effective. Trocadero was Nadja's final mention in the newspapers. After that hers was a presence of secrets.

Nadja had a habit of laughing at the wrong moment. Someone would be in the midst of telling a story, approaching a crucial point, and Nadja would begin to laugh; softly at first, then gradually increase the level of laughter to a kind of shrill cry, shocking all those present and, of course, preventing the narrator from finishing his tale. This phenomenon would not occur always, but often enough so that I would be on edge whenever we were in the company of others. Several times I was forced to escort Nadja out of the room until she regained her self-control.

The unpredictable laughter was not her only social aberration. Nadja refused to be photographed. True, photographs of Nadja do exist, but they were taken surreptitiously, without her knowledge, usually when she was drunk.

Contrary to what most of my acquaintances thought at the time, Nadja was the least mysterious person I have ever met. Everything about her was obvious. Her motives were plain, she desired love, sanity, color—all healthy pursuits. Failure on any one count can hardly be held against Nadja. Disgrace, after all, is merely a manifestation of value. The price of anything is always set in advance. Nadja made me see this. Truth is perhaps more horrible than anyone would dare admit.

She was standing there in the dream, the gun still in her hand

pointing down at the body when the cops broke in. It was Nadja
with a Barbara Stanwyck hairdo in a black robe, a silk one with
gold brocade on the wide lapels. "I shot him in the face," she
said, "and he tumbled like laundry down a chute." Those were
her exact words. They were fresh in my mind when I woke up.
The name of the movie was Riffraff, that much I could remember. But it wasn't real, it was a dream, right? I hadn't seen Nadja
in four years, and I knew who the man on the floor had to be.

One morning Nadja awoke and could not see out of her right
eye. She sent a pneumatique asking me to meet her at the Café
des Oiseaux that afternoon. "It's awful and wonderful," Nadja
said as soon as I sat down at her table. "There is a cloud in my
eye, floating across the center."

"Is it any particular color?" I asked.

"Red," said Nadja. "Like a veil of blood."

"Perhaps it is blood," I said. "Have you made arrangements to
see a doctor?"

"Doctors can only destroy," Nadja said. "Have you a cigarette?"

I gave her one, lit it and watched her blow out the smoke.

"Usually cigarette smoke is blue," she said. "Mixed with the
red it's actually quite beautiful, like two ghost ships passing
through one another on the rolling sea."

I asked Nadja what she intended to do about this problem.

"Nothing," she said. "So now I have one normal eye and one
very interesting eye. The left shall be the practical side, the ordi-

nary eye, useful and necessary. The right shall be the dream side, the indefinable, the exquisite and ungraspable. The right eye is my entrance to a drifting, unstable world ruled by color and magic. Nothing is absolute there, it is a true wilderness. Covered by this thin red veil realities are made bearable by their vagueness."

I suggested to Nadja that the presence of blood in her eye, if indeed that was what it was, might be a sign of a more serious condition, a remark that caused her to explode with laughter.

Who was Madame Sacco? Unlike Madame Blavatsky no religion was founded in her name, and also unlike the Russian she was not a charlatan. Her real name was Paulette Tanguy, born in Belleville. She set up shop as Mme. Sacco on the Rue des Usines several months after the death of her third husband, an Italian, whose name I've forgotten, though I do not believe it was Sacco. In any case, he was seldom mentioned, and neither was she very forthcoming regarding his two predecessors. As to how Mme. Sacco acquired her gift of clairvoyance, I never knew. She was never mistaken about me and I trusted her completely.

Mme. Sacco knew of Nadja's existence prior to my ever mentioning her. When Mme. Sacco told me about my preoccupation with a woman named "Hélène" I was necessarily astonished. Only a day before Nadja had said to me, seemingly apropos of nothing, "I am Hélène." These women were already connected! My reputation in certain circles for naiveté was apparently not altogether undeserved.

They did not, however, get along well. Nadja distrusted clair-
voyants—"seers" she called them, rudely. "Even if they know
what they're talking about," Nadja said, "even if their predictions
are accurate, what right have they to inform?"

Mme. Sacco sensed immediately Nadja's hostility and her performance in Nadja's presence was subdued. "There is a great deal
I could tell you about this woman," Mme. Sacco said after Nadja
had departed, "but she is opposed to it and therefore I cannot
pursue her. I do know," and here Mme. Sacco smiled, "that she is
dishonest, she feigns madness and is a danger to you."

"Do you mean," I asked, "that Nadja is sane? That she intends
to harm me?"

"Oh no," Mme. Sacco said, smiling even more handsomely
than before, "she is genuinely deranged. Her pretending is the
way she fools herself. As to harm, consider what you already do
to yourself. This Nadja is a brief disruption in your life."

Walking away from Mme. Sacco's I heard laughter coming
from above me. I looked up and saw a boy sitting on a windowsill,
playing with a live monkey. It's me, I thought. I am the monkey.

Nadja, why is it so difficult to remember exactly what you looked
like? Your precise words escape me also. My recreations are pass-
able but not accurate. You made me examine my actions, forced
me to consider possibilities other than the obvious. I am desperate now for the absolute taste of you.

I am in my studio at one minute past four o'clock in the afternoon, listening to the traffic pass in the street below my open windows. The sky is solidly gray with perhaps a stripe of white. I am embarrassed by my eagerness for night, the darkness; I never used to be.

One evening in Père Lachaise as we strolled among the graves you began to sing—some children's song, I believe—and I was horrified. I dared not mention the fact to you, knowing you would ridicule my timidity; but I could not suppress the unholy feeling I derived from your merrily singing in the cemetery. Virtually everything you did disturbed, upset, surprised me. And yet I suffer.

Wherever Nadja is must be a better place than this, especially for her. I prefer to imagine Nadja in paradise, satisfied at last with the circumstances of her existence. She could never be happy in a conventional life, better that she is allowed the latitude of feeling beyond desire. That Nadja's behavior was considered bizarre, her appearance unsightly, and that she found herself rejected on her own terms could not have given her much hope for even an acceptable afterlife.

I recall the time Nadja decided she would be an artist, a painter. She borrowed money from me for materials and did not leave her room at the Hotel Sphinx for several days. At the end of her siege Nadja emerged with one painting, which she showed to me at the Dôme. It was a self-portrait, Nadja Among the Carnivores, she called it. In the painting Nadja was depicted nude, walking in a street surrounded by ghoulish figures: huge goblins with beaks, monstrous dark shapes, devils with pitch-forks, deformed crones, a conglomeration of hideous Bosch-like characters. The style was, as one might imagine, crude, the tech-nique primitive. One could not, however, deny its power, the unsettling effect of the painting.

I told Nadja that I was impressed by the force of her work, and that I would gladly purchase the painting from her. She refused my offer. "It is not for sale," she said. "Now that you've seen it I can destroy it." I begged her not to, but at that moment she began tearing the canvas apart, shredding it into strips. "Now," Nadja said, smiling, "I have been an artist. You are my witness. I never have to prove myself again."

My feeling about Nadja is ultimately one of sadness, loss, but not without a certain degree of satisfaction in having kept faithful to my perception of her intentions. I do not pretend to have under-stood Nadja, though I remain to verify her existence.

Walking together along the Quai d'Heure Bleue on a November afternoon Nadja stopped and pointed to the river. "November is the first of the Suicide Months. Look there, in the middle of the Seine, I am drowning and boats pass oblivi-ous to my distress."

Here in the fading afternoon light, the world spinning sense-lessly as always, besieged by despair and unreasonable notions, I recall Nadja's succinct admonition, "Prepare."

Room 584,
The Starr Hotel

The Starr was a rundown transient hotel in a bad part of town. The corridor on the fifth floor was empty, dimly lit: a naked bulb hung on an exposed wire from the ceiling. Muffled noises came from a room. A disheveled-looking man in his mid-thirties appeared at the far end of the hallway. He staggered forward, feeling in his pocket for something. He looked drunk but he was not, just enormously, terribly tired. His shirt, pants and jacket were covered with dark stains. He stopped in front of a door with the numbers 584 stencilled on it. The noises grew louder and the man recognized them as those of people making love. He located a key in his pocket, took it out and looked at it. The sounds of lovemaking became even louder, more urgent. The man turned his head toward the sounds.

"Put a lid on it!" he yelled.

The lovers continued to shout and scream.

"There're laws against what you're doin'!"

The noises persisted for a few more moments, then stopped. The corridor was silent.

"*Muchas gracias,*" said the man.

He inserted the key into the lock of the door to room 584 and opened it. He went inside and closed the door behind him, leaving the key outside in the lock.

In the filthy room was a single bed, a sink with a mirror above it, a wooden chair and a small wooden dresser from which two of the drawers were missing. A torn shade was drawn down halfway over the only window, which was shut. Streetlight streamed through the window.

The man staggered over to the bed and collapsed on it, still fully dressed. He fell asleep for thirty seconds, began to snore, then woke up violently. He sat up on the edge of the bed, his feet on the floor. He rubbed his head, then scratched it hard with his left hand for a long time. After he stopped scratching, he stared at the floor. A cockroach crawled over his shoe and disappeared under the bed. His trousers were unzipped. The man pulled out his cock and inspected it closely, handling himself gently before carefully replacing his cock inside his pants and zipping up.

He stood up, stepped over to the sink and flipped a switch on the wall next to it. A fluorescent bulb blinked on above the mirror. The man inspected his face, fingering the many pock marks, turning his head first left, then right, studying his profiles. He stared straight at himself, threw back his head and spit hard at the mirror. The man smeared his saliva around on the glass with his right elbow.

Suddenly, he collapsed to the floor, barely missing hitting his chin on the porcelain sink. Lying on the floor, his body jerked spasmodically several times before he was still again. His eyes were closed. The heavy lids rose slowly.

"Thine eyes shall not see all the evil which I will bring," he said.

The man laughed, slowly, quietly at first, then louder, harder, until he coughed, curling up on the floor in a fit, his body racked by dry, painful coughing. This seizure took a full minute to subside.

Again, he spoke.

"He slew all the priests of the high places that were there...and burned men's bones."

The man climbed slowly to his feet.

"What's good?" he shouted. "Pussy and watermelon!"

He stumbled around in a circle, stopped and took out a pack of cigarettes and a book of matches from his coat pocket. He shook out a cigarette, stuck it in his mouth, lit it, then put the pack and matches back in his pocket. He stood there, smoking, rocking slowly back and forth on his big feet. The man looked at the watch on his left wrist.

"Four-thirty. Shoot. Okay, pops, got my kicks. Didn't need to be so tough on my ass, no sir. You might have learned a thing or two from your own experience."

He walked over to the sink, unzipped his pants, took out his cock and pissed into the basin. After he finished, he ran the cold water for a few seconds, turned it off and zipped up. He could hear sounds of lovemaking again.

"The devil lives in this very place," he said, "this last hotel on the moonlight mile."

The man turned away from the sink, moving mechanically, one tense muscle at a time, mumbling.

"How can Satan cast out Satan? And if Satan rise up against himself...if Satan rise...against..."

He stopped and listened. There were heavy footsteps in the corridor outside his door. Muffled voices, then silence.

The man smiled, exposing rows of green teeth.

"Oh hoo-oo-oo. Hoo-oo-oo. Oo-oo-oo," he howled. "Oh hoo-oo-oo."

His cigarette had burned down to his fingers, so he dropped it. He lit another, then went to the window and looked out. He turned away and paced back and forth, smoking, shaking his head, nodding, humming. He threw his cigarette at the window. It bounced off the glass onto the floor. The man rushed over to the window, ripped off the shade and opened it, sticking his head outside.

"The light of the body is the eye!" he shouted. "If therefore thine eye be single, thy whole body shall be full of light. But if thine eye be evil, thy whole body shall be full of darkness. If therefore the light that is in thee be darkness, how great is that darkness!"

He backed away from the window and sat down in the chair, facing the bed. He stood up, repositioned the chair so that it faced the door sat down in it again, and began to speak rapidly.

"Should have stayed on the ship, never left the ship. I still got money, though. Fucked in the ass all night long! I could be on the water, nobody know about the girls. Nobody can talk. Had to fuck the last one 'cause she looked like Pat. Pat at twenty-one. Didn't come in her until she was dead, sure she was. Can a dead girl get pregnant?"

He laughed hard and long. More light was coming in the window.

"Bitch cried and called me a demon! O Lord, thou art stronger than I, and hast prevailed. I am in derision daily, every one mocketh me."

The man stood up and again paced mechanically as he ranted.

"They cried, but there was none to save them.... Then did I beat them small as dust before the wind."

More heavy noises came from the hall. The man stared at the door as it slowly opened.

Five men entered, three in police uniforms. All five carried guns in their hands.

"Let's go," said one of the men in plainclothes. "We know you killed those nurses."

"Don't give us any more reason to shoot you," said the other plainclothesman.

"We want to shoot you," said the first plainclothesman. "Hands away from your body."

The man stood still, holding his hands out to the sides. Two of the uniformed cops swiftly handcuffed him. The plainclothesmen moved in closer and studied the man's face.

The second plainclothesman said, "You're a real monster, boy. You know that?"

"You're gonna fry," said the other one. "Sure as shit."

The man smiled, letting them see his scaly, green teeth.

"We will everyone do the imagination of his evil heart," he said.

The uniformed men escorted him out of the room.

Two Border Stories

Chuy Reyes and Esperanza Martinez are running through the desert, Chuy carrying the child. Night has fallen hard and they're cold despite the fact that they are sweating profusely. The boy is whimpering now, exhausted from crying. "Mama," he squeaks. Esperanza stops and slips to the ground.

"Come on," says Chuy, "get up. I can't carry you, too." He keeps going. Esperanza rises slowly, reluctantly. She can hear the little boy up ahead, crying louder now. Esperanza walks on. Chuy and the child, Omar, are out of sight. It's dark. Chuy shouts, there's a loud noise, someone falling, Omar screaming. Esperanza runs toward the noise. She trips over a cactus, cuts her hands on the ground. The boy is still screaming, out of control. There are several dull, thudding sounds, all in a row, then silence.

"Chuy?" Esperanza cries. "Chuy, what happened?" She gets up and makes her way slowly forward until she sees him standing in thin moonlight, empty-handed. "Chuy, where is Omar?"

Chuy kicks at a dark object, moving it toward Esperanza.

"There he is," he says. "I think he'd dead."

"Oh, Chuy, no." Esperanza kneels and turns the small, broken body so that she can see his face. "Why did you do this?" she asks.

"He was so heavy," says Chuy, "and the fuckin' kid wouldn't shut up."

"Now what do we have?" Esperanza says. "We have nothing."

"We can always get another one. Come on, help me make a hole."

Chuy begins to kick at the dirt with the heel of his right boot.

Cookie Cruz met Tico Mariposa on the Santa Fe bridge between El Paso and Juárez. She was returning from her job at the Camino Real Hotel, where she worked as a maid. Cookie lived with her mother, Rosa, in Juárez, despite the fact that she possessed a green card and could have lived in the U.S.A. Tico was born and raised in El Paso. He worked on and off as a groom at Sunland and Juárez racetracks, but had fallen in with a bad crowd that hung out at the Club Colorada in Juárez. He became a crack dealer and user. Tico was a handsome boy of twenty-two when he hit on Cookie, who was a year younger. They walked together into Mexico and that was the last anyone in El Paso ever saw of her. Tico Mariposa took Cookie Cruz with him to his room above the Buena Suerta bar on the corner of Avenue 16 de Septiembre and Pancho Villa. She was tired after working all day and not eager to make dinner for her mother and herself, so Cookie took a hit when Tico offered her one. She passed out at some point and when she woke up Tico was raping her. Cookie screamed so Tico popped her in the chops with his right fist, then smack on the nose with his left. She was bleeding and crying when Tico turned her over and tried to stick it in her ass. Cookie crawled forward, grabbed a small lamp without a shade and raked it backwards across Tico's face, shattering the bulb. He released her and Cookie jumped up. She was too dizzy from the drug to stand. Cookie fell over and looked at Tico. He was lying on his left side with pieces of the light bulb sticking out of his right eye. Cookie couldn't move from the corner where she had fallen. Her face was streaked with blood and tears. She wanted to close her eyes but they were frozen open. Tico rose to his knees and slowly picked the pieces of glass out of his face. He reached down and picked up a gun and pointed it at Cookie Cruz. She thought about Rosa, her mother, waiting for her in the little yellow house on Calle Mejia, the house her mother would never leave. Cookie had fantasized since she was fifteen about going to Nueva York and sitting in the sun on the edge of the fountain in front of the Plaza Hotel, which she'd seen a photograph of in a magazine. Cookie imagined herself standing naked in the Plaza fountain under a warm sun, and she smiled, her eyes closed, as Tico pulled the trigger.

The Big Love
of Cherry Layne

The first time Cherry Layne saw Billy Celine she thought that he was the most beautiful boy she had ever seen. Billy was then ten years old and Cherry was just eighteen. She had been hired by Billy's parents, Dorothy and Amos Celine, to babysit Billy and his younger brother, Matthew. Cherry was in her senior year of high school, Billy was in the fifth grade. He didn't really need a babysitter, but Matthew was six and their parents didn't feel comfortable leaving him alone with only Billy at home.

"You're here to watch Matt," Billy told Cherry Layne the first time she came to his house, "I can take care of myself."

"I'm sure you can," said Cherry, studying Billy's fine-featured olive-complexioned face, his large gray-green eyes staring directly at her; through her, almost. Cherry was transfixed, locking her cobalt-blue orbs on Billy; it was the birth of an obsession, the intensity of which the nubile teenager could not have imagined would one day end in unmitigated disaster.

Cherry became the Celine boys' regular babysitter, even on weekends when she could have gone on dates with boys from her school. Cherry was a beautiful, intelligent girl but she was not what could be considered popular among her classmates. The boys who asked her out were politely but firmly refused, and they were not encouraged to try again. The other girls thought Cherry odd in that she rarely chose to participate in either sporting or scholastic extracurricular events, disappearing quickly each day after classes were over. The fact that she was unfailingly polite in a straightforward, unaffected manner forced her classmates if not to respect her, to at least defer to her obvious desire to be left alone.

The truth was that Cherry Layne was almost fatally shy. She often felt faint after warding off another student's attempt to engage her in some way. Somehow she managed to remain outwardly pleasant while secretly shrivelling. Cherry would regularly repair to the privacy of a toilet stall in the girls bathroom following such a confrontation and force herself to breathe deeply at regular intervals for several minutes until she had regained a semblance of composure and could once again "pass among the living," as she wrote in the diary discovered after her death.

Cherry was an only child, born to Norman and Gretchen Layne when both were in their late thirties. The Laynes were attentive rather than particularly loving parents, preoccupied as they were by their work as biochemists at the local university. Due to their long hours in the laboratory—Norman and Gretchen were a research team specializing in the effects of temperature shifts on bodily functions—their daughter spent most of her early years in daycare situations. Cherry's aversion to collective activities was noted and remarked upon by a number of her supervisors but the Laynes were undisturbed by this observation, assuming that Cherry must, like them, be preoccupied by her own personal agenda. They were, of course, somewhat curious as to what that might be, but not to the point of challenging her behavior in order to find out.

Had the Laynes known the nature of Cherry's innermost being, no doubt they would have made an effort to facilitate her social life. She did well at school and earned money babysitting on the weekends, an occupation she enjoyed, feeling far less shy, if not entirely confident, when dealing with young children. The children whom Cherry tended unfailingly responded to her in a positive manner, the Celine boys being no exception.

Billy Celine at ten years old was already something of a terror among his peers. At school teachers identified him as the ringleader of a group of boys who singled out bullies, boys who gave those students weaker than themselves a hard time, and proceeded to collectively administer to them a severe beating and otherwise terrorize them until their behavior improved.

When confronted by school authorities regarding these vigilante tactics, Billy refused to identify a single one of his accomplices; nor would he admit to even a passing knowledge of the activities he stood accused of organizing. Billy's intractability was, of course, brought to the attention of his parents, but, as Amos Celine informed his son's inquisitors, without sufficient

proof—the testimony of his wounded accuser notwithstanding—
the possibility of litigation directed towards the school district
and its administrators was certainly not out of the question, end-
ing the matter for the time being.

Billy was thereafter monitored on a regular basis at school.
Privately, Amos confronted his oldest son at home, and advised
him that while Billy's intentions may have seemed reasonable
in a frontier justice sort of way, this penchant for violent retri-
bution would inevitably lead to real calamity. Billy Celine listened carefully to his father, whom he loved and trusted, and
replied with a polite "Yes, sir." In truth, Amos Celine's admon-
ishment made no large impression upon his son's opinion.
Billy remained determined to redress perceived transgressions,
however, wherever and whenever he saw fit, a pattern of
behavior that continued unabated until the moment of his
premature death.

As the years passed, Cherry and Billy grew closer, becoming friends despite their age difference. The Celines employed
Cherry to babysit Matthew even as Billy matured, not wanting
to burden him with the responsibility, but also because they
had grown extremely fond of the girl, coming to think of her
almost as a daughter due to the amount of time she spent at
their house.

Billy and Cherry, however, did not at any time conceive of
their relationship as that of brother and sister. At first, Billy
pretended to resent her presence, fearing his friends might

think he, as well as his younger brother, was in her charge. Secretly, though, Billy was always glad to see her. He had felt stirrings of a sexual nature since the age of five; at least that was when he first became aware of his urges due to occasional nocturnal emissions. Billy began masturbating at the age of six, and ever since Cherry Layne had shown up she had become, unbeknownst to her, a frequent fantasy participant in his onanistic activities.

Cherry, of course, was as enamored of Billy as it was possible for an eighteen-year-old girl to be of a ten-year-old boy. Their actual contact, of course, was limited to somewhat cryptic conversation; each eyed the other warily, like wolves slinking about the perimeter of a human encampment. As the years passed Billy became bolder around Cherry; when he was twelve he began asking her about her boyfriends. When she told him that she didn't have any, Billy accused her of lying to him.

"Why should I lie to you?" she asked.

"You're twenty years old," he said. "You must go on dates."

Cherry looked Billy directly in the eyes, and said, "I'm waiting for the right boy to come along."

On the night of Billy's thirteenth birthday, Cherry, who had been invited to the Celine house for cake and ice cream, slipped him a small envelope when his parents weren't looking. When he began to say something, Cherry covered his mouth with her right hand and slid it into his pocket.

Later that night, alone in his room, Billy looked inside the envelope. He found a photograph of Cherry Layne in which she lay naked on a bed, smiling. Billy called Cherry on the telephone that night for the first time.

"Thanks for the picture," he told her. "It's the best gift I got."

"I thought you'd like it."

"Probably I'd like the real thing more."

"We could find out."

"You comin' tomorrow night?"

"No, day after. Your folks're goin' to a movie."

"Then's soon enough, I guess."

"Good night, Billy. Happy birthday again."

"Thanks. See ya."

Two nights later, after Amos and Dorothy Celine left, Cherry watched television for a half-hour with Matthew, then read him a story before putting him to bed. Matthew always fell asleep quickly, and this night was no exception.

Billy was lying on the bed in his room reading Tarzan and the Jewels of Opar when Cherry Layne knocked on his door.

"Come in," he said.

Cherry entered and saw Billy wearing only his undershorts. She walked over and sat down next to him on the bed. Billy tossed Tarzan and the Jewels of Opar on the floor and sat up. Cherry touched the top of his head with her right hand, then his left ear before stroking his chest. Billy had an erection, which he quickly covered with his left hand. Cherry took his hand away and pulled off Billy's shorts, then pushed him down. She squeezed his cock and he came immediately. Cherry laughed, bent her head down and licked the come off her hand and the head of his penis. Cherry stood up and took off all her clothes, then lay down next to Billy.

"How long do you think it'll take before your thing can get hard again?" she asked.

Billy began to masturbate himself and in less than a minute he was half erect. Cherry pulled him over on top of her and spread her legs. They kissed with their mouths closed for a while before Cherry felt Billy's hard-on stretched flat on her stomach. She reached down and guided him into her. He didn't say anything, only grunted as Cherry placed one of her hands on each cheek of his ass and pulled.

"Try not to come," she whispered into his left ear, "until I tell you to."

Cherry and Billy made love this way for several months until one night his parents returned earlier than expected, heard unusual noises coming from Billy's room and discovered them. Neither Cherry nor Billy said anything to the Celines. She got up, got dressed, left the house and never came back. Billy refused to talk about it; despite threats of punishment by Amos and Dorothy. Matthew wanted to know why Cherry didn't come to the house anymore. His parent just told him that she was too busy with her schoolwork to babysit or visit.

Billy became a stranger to the other members of his family. He went to school as usual but both his teachers and his friends felt that he was almost a different person—distant, uncommunicative. Nobody, other than his parents, knew about the situation with Cherry Layne. Amos and Dorothy decided not to talk to Norman and Gretchen Layne about it after Billy threatened to kill both them and himself if they did. The Celines told Billy they would honor his request if he agreed never to see Cherry Layne again. They chose to interpret his silence as assent.

Billy and Cherry, however, met as often as possible, their rendezvous occuring most frequently in the woods that surrounded the town. They were careful never to be seen together. After Cherry had graduated from high school she surprised and dismayed her parents by turning down scholarship offers from several prestigious universities, enrolling instead at the local college. Unbeknownst to Gretchen and Norman, of course, was that remaining close to Billy Celine was her main reason for doing so.

On the evening of her 22nd birthday, Cherry told Billy that she thought that she was pregnant. Her parents had presented her with a new red Saturn automobile that afternoon and they talked as they cruised the less traveled roads through the forest.

"We'll need money," said Cherry. "I've got a little."

"I'll get some more," Billy promised.

"How?" Cherry asked.

"I'm the man," he said. "Let me worry about it."

The couple agreed to meet the following day at noon, each of them bringing only what they considered items indispensible to their flight. Neither of them were to leave a farewell note to their respective parents or friends.

Four days later the following item appeared in newspapers across the country:

FUGITIVE YOUTH KILLS SELF, BABYSITTER IN CHASE

Nacogdoches, Texas—A 14-year-old boy fled from Crowley, Louisiana, to Texas with his former babysitter, then killed her and himself during a police chase, authorities said yesterday.

William Celine and Cherry Layne, 22, held up the Moor Hotel in Sheik, Louisiana, where they had spent the previous night posing as sister and brother. They robbed the desk clerk at gunpoint and fled in a red car, police said.

Texas Highway Patrolmen were attempting to stop the car when Celine opened fire on them. Celine then shot Layne in the head before turning the gun on himself, authorities said. The weapon was registered in Louisiana to the boy's father. Their car crashed into a light pole. An autopsy showed that Layne, who was driving, died instantly.

Nacogdoches Police Lieutenant Enrico Lago said yesterday that Layne, a college student who lived with her parents, didn't try to alert authorities. "We're not ruling out a possible romantic relationship," he said.

A Really
Happy Man

When I was a boy in Chicago during the 1950s, there was a man who lived on our street named Fred Biderman. Mr. Biderman was a short, bald man with a thick brown mustache that served as a line of demarcation, as if his pleasant, perpetually smiling face were divided into two different countries: Upper Biderman, dominated by twin black orbs, a sun and moon in states of permanent eclipse; and Lower Biderman, bordered on the north by the hirsute forest, and featuring a curving pink and red two-lane road running east and west above the pock-marked cliff of Biderman's mountainous chin.

Mr. Biderman, who was in his late forties and early fifties when I knew him, was a butcher. He had a small shop on the main commercial avenue a few blocks away from a five-room bungalow in which he lived alone. I'd been told by someone that his mother had lived with him until she died, but I don't recall ever meeting or seeing her. Fred Biderman's only obvious passion was for old British sportscars. He owned two MG convertibles which he parked in front of his house and on which he labored weekends. He rarely drove the cars but when he did his smile seemed even broader than usual as he motored slowly along, waving at the neighbors.

Virtually all of the women on our block patronized Mr. Biderman's butcher shop; everyone seemed to like him. One day a man walked into Biderman's market and handed him a business card. The man introduced himself as an advertising executive, told Mr. Biderman that he had an interesting face, and asked the butcher to give him a call if he felt like exploring the possibility of working for him. Soon after this, Mr. Biderman was hired by the man's firm to promote a brand of cigarettes. Fred Biderman's beaming face began appearing on billboards all over the city under the words "They'll Make You Feel Better." An unusual aspect of this campaign was that the poster did not show Mr. Biderman smoking a cigarette; there was the butcher's mirthful image next to a picture of a pack of cigarettes. The truth, of course, was that Fred Biderman did not smoke, nor, apparently, had he ever.

After several months as a billboard icon, Mr. Biderman closed his butcher shop. His face appeared with other products, always the same, grinning like the most contented man in the universe, which at this time in his life he may have been. He even appeared on television, promoting merchandise as diverse as mops and brooms, paint, milk and towels. People in the neighborhood lamented the closing of Biderman's butcher shop but nobody could begrudge him the opportunity to improve his financial well-being merely by dint of utilizing the same smile they had grown used to seeing hovering above a rosy display of raw hamburger.

As Mr. Biderman's income grew, he began to acquire more old British sportscars, most of them non-functional. He parked them on the street where they remained, immobile, subject to his availability and inclination to work on them. The neighbors started complaining about his automobiles taking up too many parking places. Men returning home from work in the evening often had to park their cars a block away or more. Mr. Biderman, no longer the amiable butcher with a reasonable hobby, was suddenly spoken of from house to house as a selfish person. His smile, I heard my friend Anthony Tonino's mother say, was not really an expression of his feelings: It was a facial condition caused by unnaturally short muscles around his mouth. Mr. Biderman, she said, had no choice but to smile due to this involuntary physical contortion. Where Mrs. Tonino got this information I never knew, but it was more than evident that the smiling butcher—at least we'd all thought that he was smiling—was no longer considered a friend to all.

Mr. Biderman soon thereafter sold his house and moved away. I never learned to which neighborhood he'd relocated himself and his dozen or so seldom-exercised sportscars, but once in a great while he would drive one of them down the avenue past where his butcher shop had been. From his little cockpit Mr. Biderman would wave to us as he puttered by, a big grin on his face as usual.

After this residents of the block were relieved to be able to park their cars closer to their homes. However, as the local economy improved, families began acquiring second and even third vehicles. Parking on the street again became a problem, and this time Mr. Biderman's face was nowhere to be seen except next to a box of crackers or detergent or a milk carton.

By the time I graduated from high school Fred Biderman had disappeared from public view altogether. Nobody seemed to know what had happened to him or why his image no longer graced our billboards and television screens. Perhaps he just became wealthy enough that he could quit the advertising business as he had the meat market. One thing I was reasonably certain of, however, was that if he were still alive and able he was tinkering away on a decrepit but cute tiny car, appearing to all who saw him—Mrs. Tonino's information notwithstanding—to be a really happy man.

The Brief Confession of an Unrepentant Erotic

My real name is Julius Mordecai Pincus. I am a Jew, born in the small Balkan village of Vidin, in Bulgaria, on March 31, 1885. I was the seventh of eight children, and I grew up mostly in Bucharest and Vienna. I attended school from the age of ten until I was sixteen. At seventeen I began life on my own, living first in Budapest, then Vienna, Munich and Berlin. It was during this initial stage of independent discovery, roughly from 1902 to 1905, that I recreated myself.

At sixteen I was initiated into the rites of male/female sexual relations by a woman of fifty. Prominent in Viennese society, Anna was a wealthy, not altogether unattractive widow. She paid me to visit her; she had employed a number of other boys before it came my turn. Though Anna was well-schooled in a variety of forms of lovemaking, she preferred the oral type. She told me she was and had been since the age of eleven a chronic masturbator, an activity she enjoyed performing for her lovers.

I suppose my fascination with women's bodies began with Anna. She had a full, well-preserved figure, rather thick-legged. Above the nipple of her left breast was a large, dark blue, star-shaped mole. Anna referred to it as her "Egyptian wound," or "the Pharaoh's kiss."

From Anna I went on to discover the delights of Celeste. Del'Al, Mary, Hermine, Lucy, Marcelle, Claudine, Mireille, Cesarine, Andrée, Mado, Henriette, Clara, Lydis, Simone, Geneviève, Hilda, Marianne, Jeanette, Suzette, Aischa, Eliane, Paquita, Dinitia, Odile, Odette, Cleo and others whose names do not come immediately to mind. They were and are all wonderful simply because they are women. Women are the greatest of all wonders, the most fascinating of God's secrets. Of course, I believe in God. I have always believed in God. It is God who enables me to breathe into life and death these paintings and drawings, who works my wrist and fingers, stimulates my brain, unpeels my eyes.

It is almost morning. I am sitting at the writing table in my bedroom at the Villa des Camellias. I know now that I am unable to go on. As I remarked yesterday afternoon to Dubreuil, I have worked so hard, only to be considered a freak, at best a beast, at worst a fraud. Shall I be obliged to suffer further deprecations by the pens and lips of failed artists and frightened, self-loathing weasels? I think not.

This is my brief confession. My public and private life will be remembered and memorialized by Hermine and Lucy, the only two women I have ever truly loved. My physical life is finally in my own hands. I own the future, which is as unenviable a responsibility as anyone could imagine. But this is the "time of tongue between the teeth," as the Cuban Indians say.

I have never been a man until now. Women with fingers between their legs, spectacular tropical sunsets, a red ribbon lying in the street. Who else but I can decide what is meaningful?

Critics accuse me of drawing dirty pictures, depicting women disrespectfully, in uncouth fashion. They're fools. I have absolute reverence for these women. I am fascinated by them, astounded by their honesty and ability to survive despite a variety of cruelties having been imposed upon them. I am not so brave. And so I regard these women with admiration, inspect their habitats, closely observe and record their habits, postures, uninhibited instants, as would any proper anthropologist.

The sisters Odile and Odette, my closest companions of late, are perhaps the most perfect examples of this particular study. When they were six and four, respectively, they were raped by their father, who continued to practice upon them diverse sexual abuse until Odile, at the age of eleven, stabbed him to death while he slept. The girls were institutionalized for five years, raised by nuns and then released into the world, virtually penniless, to make their way. I discovered them a couple of years later.

Odile was a prostitute and Odette worked as a washerwoman, mopping up barrooms. I took them in and employed them as models. Their figures are superb and each is unrestrained in her lovemaking. In this regard they are more than I can handle. They need constant attention and to engage in sexual activities several times a day. I offer them to my friends regularly and so manage to please everyone.

Odile and Odette remind me of the chocolatas of Cuba, las negritas, with their full lips and taunting gazes. I was happy in Cuba; the tropical light is like no other, the foliage as dense and dazzlingly beautiful as any I've seen. A kind of reptilian mystery pervades the atmosphere, a suggestion of danger slithers through the mind and is reflected in the movements of the people. These sisters of mine, were they dark instead of blonde, if they spoke rapid Spanish rather than languid French, could be Lupe and Luisa in place of Odile and Odette.

In Munich, when I was eighteen, I met a wonderful girl named Liebe—Love—whose father raised flowers. Liebe and I would wander among the flowers, touching hands, stopping here and there to kiss, and finally, finding an appropriate place and being unable to restrain ourselves any longer, we would collapse among the reds, yellows, blues, greens, violets.

During this time I worked for Simplicissimus, a satirical review, and decided to anagrammatize my name from Pincus to Pascin. It was then that I came upon the works of Klimt and

Schiele, and realized how one might approach erotica tenderly and with humor. This was the path I chose to follow, portraying the sudden danger of lust and risking the harsh criticism that often ensues when one attempts to entertain.

My arrival in Paris on Christmas Eve of 1905 coincided, more or less, with others I felt were of a similar disposition. Among these were Libermann, Modigliani, Picasso, Kisling and my fellow landsmen Soutine and Chagall. Each of them expressed in those days a desire to create holiness out of vulgarity. I have sought to do the same—in Munich, Berlin, Paris, New Orleans, Florida, Texas, Havana, New York, Tunis; in dance bars, offices, brothels, studios, cafés; with ink, charcoal, paint, pencil. My objective has been to delineate the perfect within the imperfect. I would not compromise in subject or form. A man's temperament is more important than his work.

I want to say that I am not evil, that I have never had an evil thought, but I don't know if this can ever be true of any person other than those born demented. I have manipulated, coerced, flattered falsely, given incorrect information, misrepresented myself, and none of this in the name of Art. What living being can deny in his soul that he has done the same?

I have been unable to marry the woman I love because she will not divorce her husband and I will not divorce my wife. Life drags on and one attempts to ignore the inevitable, to disguise ugliness, pretend not to be affected by ridicule and calumny, not recognize the symptoms of serious illness. All at once, it seems, one must succumb. My insistent attempts at immortality have resulted in a body of work anyone can contemplate without interference from interpretation.

This is a cold night and I am alone. Odile and Odette await me at the café. Faint flakes of snow swirl outside the window in which Paquita's painted face and breasts are reflected. Life itself is inadequate for my requirements. I am a demanding, selfish, foolish creature, no better than a hungry dog. Mine is a deserving fate. Poverty is hideous, madness is concrete. I am done with this at last! I am done.

No man, and above all no artist, should live for more than forty-five years. If by then he has not already given his best, he will achieve nothing more after that age. There is no cure for this relentless, self-inflicted terror. It is ultimately an artificial life. Reality is what remains.

The Yellow Palace

My name is Antonio Pulli. I am seventy-six years old in this year of 1406 by the Arabic calendar. For the past three and a half decades I have operated a restaurant in Cairo. For a quarter of a century prior to that my main occupation was as companion and aide to Farouk, the former king of Egypt. I was known popularly as Farouk's procurer, mainly of women. While it is true that in his mature years Farouk maintained a sizeable appetite for women, many of whom I assisted him in locating, our association began when I was sixteen and he was eight years old. My father, Francesco Pulli, was the court electrician at Rasel-Tin Palace in Alexandria during the reign of Farouk's father, Sultan Fuad. I repaired a toy train of Farouk's and from that day forward we were inseparable.

I was eventually knighted by Farouk—a bey in Arabic—and there was nothing of his activities to which I was not privy until the moment of his exile, at which time I was imprisoned by the rebels. They broke into my quarters at Abdin Palace and discovered the glass case containing thirty hooks on each of which hung a key appended with a tag detailing the name of a particular woman, her address and a description of the entrance to her house. Among these keys were several to rooms at Cairo hotels, such as the Semiramis and the Heliopolis House. That Farouk enjoyed the company of women is undeniable. I would estimate that during his lifetime he consorted in one fashion or another with more than five thousand women, more than even his revered grandfather, Farouk's idol, Ismail the Magnificent. Farouk was unrivalled in the pursuit of his libidinous pastime. An example: When he built al-Moussa Hospital in Alexandria he had constructed on the top floor seventeen lavishly furnished rooms, each with a grand view of the Mediterranean, solely in order to have a private place to bring his women. Never have I seen a place where the contrast of suffering and pleasure was so immediately evident.

It would be too easy, however, to dismiss Farouk as a selfish, shallow man or an unfeeling ruler. He was probably not mistaken when he said to me and Mohammed Hassan, his Nubian chauffeur, shortly before his final departure for Capri, "In this country of twenty million souls, I do not have a single friend." But there are reasons for this, and the fault lies not solely with Farouk himself. Mohammed Hassan, who has for many years now operated a hotel at Khartoum in the Sudan, could testify to this as well. Farouk's life might have been entirely different had he not had to assume the crown at the age of sixteen.

When Farouk was a boy he displayed sincere interest in academic areas: the sciences, literature, music. At fifteen he was sent to England to complete his education. Farouk studied at the Royal Military Academy at Woolwich, where he was attended by four men from the Sultan's court: Ahmed Mohammed Hassanein Bey, the Minister Plenipotentiary; General Aziz el-Misri Pasha, a military adviser; Saleih Hashim, professor of Arabic and Islamic science; and Dr. Kafrawi, his personal physician. All of these men reported that Farouk was acquitting himself admirably at school. Farouk was a good horseman, and he spoke fluent French and English, in addition to Arabic. He represented Egypt at the funeral of King George V while he was in England, and the reports were that his behavior in that circumstance was exemplary. I have no doubt that had Farouk been able to develop gradually his own personality he would have become a respected and generous king.

Sultan Fuad died barely a year after Farouk left for England. He was brought back immediately after his father's death and was forced to assume the kingdom of Mohammed Ali, the Great, the Father of modern Egypt, hereditary Vizier of Egypt and Governor of Nubia, Sennar, Kordofan and Darfur. Mohammed Ali's grandson, Ismail, expanded the kingdom; it was Ismail who built an opera house and commissioned Giuseppe Verdi to write Aida. Fuad was Ismail's son, and he did not prepare Farouk adequately for the role of king. The Egypt over which Farouk assumed leadership was one rampant with disease: tuberculosis, malaria and syphilis were common. Babies' eyes were covered with sores and flies. Unfaithful wives were cut up and thrown into the Nile; peasant women would eat the polluted Nile mud as part of their religious belief that it would assure easy childbirth, and they would smear the mud on their bodies as a sign of sorrow following the death of a loved one. These practices spread bacterial disease such as bilharzia and hookworm. Primitive as Egypt appears now, it was then even more so.

Farouk, of course, had grown up in luxurious circumstances, mainly at Ras-el-Tin Palace. His mother, Queen Nazli, was a Franco-Egyptian, the eldest daughter of Abdul Rahim Sabri, and she had been raised in Paris. Farouk's nursemaid, a Turkish woman named Ah'sha Galshan, had been carefully chosen for her bountiful breasts. She used often to complain about Farouk's powerful jaw that left her nipples sore! Biting women's nipples remained one of Farouk's greatest pleasures. It was Ah'sha Galshan and the assistant court chamberlain, Ahmed Hassanein Pasha, who raised the young Farouk. The Sultan was thirty years older than Queen Nazli, and neither of them paid much attention to the future king.

Fuad lay in state in Cairo at the Mosque el-Rifai, where Farouk accepted the condolences and best wishes of world leaders. He took up residence in Abdin Palace at sixteen. Mohammed Altabii, an Egyptian journalist, wrote of Farouk at that time: "He acquires admiration and respect for his person, without resource to his crown. He is intellectually mature, has vast culture, and is well-spoken in public. The love of the people for Farouk rises daily, and this from a people that has always been disappointed in its leaders. Only Farouk has not disappointed them." And the Prime Minister of Lebanon declared Farouk "not only the king of Egypt, but the King of all the Arabs."

Egypt in the 1930s, of course, was occupied by the British, and Farouk had to learn how to deal with this presence in the face of fierce Moslem objection. Nazli had no love for the Arab masses; being half French, she considered herself a European, and spent much of her time in Paris and Switzerland. Farouk's four sisters—Fawzia, who would later become the first wife of the Shah of Iran, Faiza, Faika and Fathia—knew nothing of the world. Farouk had to depend entirely on his father's advisers, who, naturally, counselled the young monarch to leave the administration of the government to them.

So Farouk found himself with a kingdom to amuse himself in. He enlisted me as his "right-hand man," as the Americans say. Along with Mohammed Hassan as chauffeur, Pietro della Valle, the palace assistant barber, and two Albanian bodyguards, I was closest to Farouk. We comprised the king's coterie, his most trusted servants. When he was seventeen, Farouk married Safinaz, who was only fifteen, and whose name he changed to Farida, in keeping with his father Fuad's policy of beginning names of royalty with the letter F. Farida was coerced into the marriage by her parents. She did not want to marry Farouk, and told me before the wedding, "I have read the story of Joan of Arc and I feel the same as she when she knew that she would be burned at the stake the next day."

The marriage was a disaster. Both Farouk and Farida were far too young to understand what a marriage was supposed to be, so they ended up living very separate lives. That Farida bore Farouk only daughters and not a son did not help matters. And when Farouk's mother, Nazli, entered into an at-first secret marriage with Ahmed Hassanein, Farouk's view of the trustworthiness of women plummeted to an unrecoverable depth.

Farouk's biggest problem, in his own mind at least, was the diminutive size of his penis. Though Farouk was six feet tall and of muscular proportions as a young man, his penis, when fully erect, measured no more than two inches in length. This fact, perhaps more than any other, contributed to his obsession with sex. As he grew fatter over the years, exceeding three hundred pounds by the age of thirty, it became virtually impossible for Farouk to successfully have sexual intercourse with a woman. Annie Berrier, a French showgirl who resided for a time in Cairo, explained to Farouk that there were methods other than intercourse by which a woman might be satisfied. It was due to Annie Berrier that Farouk acquired the nickname "Talented Tongue." This appellation pleased Farouk enormously; he made no secret of his indebtedness to Annie for educating him in the more sophisticated forms of lovemaking. Farouk told me that with Annie it was even possible for him to enjoy so-called normal sexual congress. Apparently she was extraordinarily adept at the act, managing to accomplish with Farouk what few others could. The King spoke highly of her always and was deeply saddened when she returned to France.

During World War II, Farouk became convinced that the British would lose. Though he had been educated in England and affected various British mannerisms, especially in speech, Farouk felt that Rommel's Afrika Korps and Graziani's Italian armies could not be defeated. Farouk often inveighed against the swaggering, racist Australian and New Zealand troops that were stationed in Egypt. These soldiers treated the Egyptian citizens like dogs, with no respect whatsoever, and ignored entirely the Egyptian officers. This insolence infuriated Farouk. He could not forget the saying, "In Egypt the only power above Allah is the British." It was this that compelled Farouk to enter into a secret agreement with Hitler that would allow Rommel to occupy the country. Hitler dispatched Joseph Goebbels to visit Farouk and work out a plan. The British, after all, had deposed Ismail the Magnificent, and not one Egyptian had raised a hand or a voice in his defense. Farouk was eager to enlist Nazi support in his desire for revenge. This, as it turned out, was not to be, and so Farouk privately vowed to find another way to expel the British. It is to his credit that British forces withdrew from Cairo and Alexandria in 1947, and evacuated Egyptian territory altogether two years later. The Moslem movement provided the force, certainly, but it was Farouk who supplied the necessary push.

Farouk had many internal enemies. The fiercest among them without question was Wahid Yusri, who also became Farida's lover. Farouk was incensed about this, even though he was madly in love at this time with the Princess Fatima Toussan, the wife of Prince Hassan Toussan, a wealthy nobleman twenty-two years her senior. The prince spent most of his time tending to his thoroughbred racehorses and so allowed Fatima ample opportunity to meet with Farouk.

Yusri and Nahas Pasha, Farouk's other archenemy, combined to make the king's political life miserable. I will never forget the February day in 1945 when the Prime Minister, Ahmed Maher Pasha, was assassinated by a young revolutionary named Mahmud el-Isawi. Farouk, who was in the process of creating the Arab League, was convinced that Yusri was behind the killing. He stormed into Farida's bedroom and vowed to cut out her vagina. Farida bore Farouk three daughters, the last of whom, also named Farida, Farouk vehemently denied having fathered. He was frustrated in his desire for a male heir, and upset that he had no blood relative to support him in his battles.

Farouk's closest friend outside the court was the former King of Albania, Ahmed Zog. Zog and Farouk met almost nightly after the war at The Scarabee, a small Cairo nightclub. It was King Zog who introduced Farouk to the actress Nadia Gray, whose real name was Princess Cantacuzino. Farouk's attempt at seducing this woman, who would become a movie star for Federico Fellini and other European directors, was a failure, and he accused Zog of poisoning her against him. Zog pointed out that it was he who had introduced Farouk to her in the first place, and berated Farouk for thinking ill of him. It was not customary for Farouk to apologize to anyone for anything he may have said or done, but he begged Zog's forgiveness for this unreasonable act. Only Zog could elicit this kind of humble behavior from Farouk.

It was Zog, too, who chided Farouk about his excesses at the gaming tables. Farouk kept a reserved seat at the tout va—no limit—table at the Monte Carlo casino. In Cairo he played chemin de fer regularly at the Royal Automobile Club on Kasr-en-Nil Street, he gambled in Cannes and Deauville; and he kept a faithful record of his losses. In one year alone Farouk lost 850,000 Egyptian pounds, at that time—1947—equivalent to two million American dollars. Farouk casually remarked to Zog that he, Farouk, had even gambled with the throne and won. Zog replied that one may lose many times at poker but a throne can be lost but once. Farouk then stated: "In ten years there will be only five kings left in the world. The king of clubs, the king of diamonds, the king of hearts, the king of spades and the King of England."

Farouk divorced Farida at the same time that he forced the Shah of Iran to divorce Fawzia. Farouk hated Reza Pahlavi; he thought him personally dishonest and despised Pahlavi's father, who had previously taken asylum in South Africa. Farouk wanted no connection with the Shah. Farouk's own intention was to marry Princess Fatima but she betrayed him by marrying Prince Juan Orleans Bractara in Paris. This marriage sent Farouk into a berserk rage. He took a cane and stomped around the palace, smashing vases and furniture. He never recovered completely from this loss. Fatima was one woman he could not claim, and it galled him.

At this same time, in the late forties, Huda Sha'rawi died. She was the wife of the President of Egypt's first parliament, and in 1919 was the first woman to discard the veil. She was the leader of women's emancipation in Egypt and, strange as it may seem, Farouk revered her. It seemed to Farouk that his world was crumbling. Other than Zog, Farouk felt he could trust no one beyond his closest aides, such as Pietro, Mohammed Hassan and me.

Farouk began spending more time on his yacht, the Fakhr-al-Behar, and at his house on the east bank of the Nile at Helwan, a cozy place named Roken el-Farouk ("Farouk's little corner") at which he kept rendezvous with women. He developed a taste for hashish mixed with honey, and was often unavailable for official duties for two or three days at a time. Farouk joked that the only palace he belonged in was the "yellow palace," which in Egypt is a name for the insane asylum.

Then Farouk met and married Narriman Sadek, who in 1951, the year of their marriage, was sixteen years old. She bore him his only son, Prince Said, and though their marriage was no more satisfactory in other ways than Farouk's union with Farida, he remained beholden to Narriman for having produced Said. Farouk announced to me on the night of Said's birth that he could now die happily, knowing he had earned the respect of his ancestors, particularly Ismail.

Farouk's weight continued to rise, and his preoccupations with gambling, women and drugs increased in intensity. Pietro della Valle and I feared for his sanity, and one evening in 1951 he declared us Egyptian citizens, despite our having been born in Italy. Being Catholic, neither of us had been circumcised as Moslem boys are at the age of thirteen. Farouk demanded that we be circumcised, though both of us were almost forty. We were forced by Farouk to undergo this extremely painful ceremony, and it was after this that I began to distance myself from him.

Farouk created a Black Brigade à la the Swiss Guards; Sudanese soldiers, each of whom was over six feet tall, were enlisted as a personal bodyguard. He felt endangered by the Moslem Brotherhood, an organization that wanted Egypt to declare war on England. Riots broke out in all of the cities. The Black Brigade was soon disbanded due to outbreaks among them of syphilis and other diseases. Farouk complained to me again and again that he was friendless and unloved, and I could not contradict him.

On July 26, 1952, the day Farouk abdicated the throne and he and Narriman boarded the Mahroussa in Alexandria to sail for Capri, I was arrested. I never saw Farouk again. I know that he at first took up residence at the Eden Paradise Hotel in Annacapri, commanding forty rooms in which to house his entourage. Farouk next ensconced himself at Frascati, south of Rome, and later, after Narriman left him and resettled with Said in Lausanne, he moved into Rome. It was there that Farouk made the acquaintance of the gangster Lucky Luciano, also in exile, who informed Farouk that there was a price on my former master's head of $140,000. Farouk knew there were many men—and probably women, too—who would gladly have him assassinated, so he never went anyplace thereafter without his Albanian bodyguards.

The end was sordid, of course. Farouk weighed more than twenty-three stone, 320 pounds. He gambled heavily, as always. Pietro remained with him and informed me later that Farouk carried a black 6.35 caliber Beretta automatic, along with pills for kidney problems and high blood pressure. I can remember when he was forced to undergo an operation for hemorrhoids; it was so painful that afterwards he made Zog promise to have the doctor killed.

Farouk's sexual appetite in his last years, according to Pietro, was for overweight women with large breasts and wide hips. Heavyset call girls flocked to Rome and Monte Carlo in the hope of becoming one of his favorites. I recall Farouk saying often that only a woman's ankles determined whether or not she was beautiful.

Pietro said that Farouk died of heart failure after devouring his third dinner of an evening, this last having included seven chickens, a candied ham, a dozen baked potatoes, a pot of rice, several chocolate eclairs, a Sacher torte, some kind of flaming dessert, two bottles of wine and many cups of espresso. He had just lit one of his custom-wrapped Havana cigars, a Monte Cristo, I'm sure, when he keeled over and banged his head on the table. Farouk's last words, uttered to a prostitute he had hired for the night, were, "When the cow falls, a thousand knives appear." This is an old Egyptian proverb meaning he had no real friends, and no one to defend his memory after his death. Farouk was forty-five years old.

Salam alaikum.

For This, We Give Thanks

My most memorable Thanksgiving occurred one year in the early 1980s when I received a phone call late in the afternoon from my friend Don Ellis. Don lived several blocks away from me at that time and when I was informed that he was on the line, I assumed he was about to invite me to his house for a drink that evening.

"Do you hear that?" Don shouted at me after I had said hello. "They're cutting a hole in my living-room wall!"

"Who's cutting a hole?" I shouted back in order to be heard over the sounds of what I clearly recognized as buzzing chainsaws encountering substantial resistance.

"The fire department," said Don. "Smoke was coming from the wall around the fireplace, so we called the fire department and now they're cutting it down."

"That's terrible," I said.

"Yeah, there are twenty-two people here waiting for dinner watching my house being destroyed. I'm drinking my best Scotch. Can you come over and carve the turkey? I'm already too drunk to do it."

"I'll be there in ten minutes."

I told my family what was happening at Don's, grabbed my coat and said I'd be back as soon as I could to carve our own turkey. The scene at Don's house was even more bizarre than I imagined. Not only were there large pieces missing from the front wall, but as darkness fell it had begun to snow and flakes were swirling in the smoky livingroom. An increasingly insistent wind drove the snow inside, forcing Don's family and guests to put on coats and hats.

This reminded me of the famously beautiful scene in director Carol Reed's movie Odd Man Out, when Robert Newton, as the crazed artist, Lukey, attempts to paint a portrait of the virtually inert Irish rebel Johnny McQueen as King Lear while McQueen is bleeding to death from a gunshot wound, snowflakes streaming through the tattered, half-gone roof of a Dublin tenement and settling on dying Johnny's sainted head.

By the time I arrived at Don's, everybody was drinking whiskey. Don was in the kitchen propped up against the refriger-ator, a long woollen plaid scarf wrapped around his neck, swig-ging from a bottle of 18-year-old Macallan's. A television was on nearby and Vivaldi's "Four Seasons" was piping from the stereo.

As soon as I entered the kitchen, Don's wife, Kathleen, hand-ed me a tumbler full of whiskey. She then uncovered an enor-mous roasted turkey that had been cooling on a cutting board. I took a healthy sip from the tumbler, set it down on a countertop, picked up the large carving knife and fork that Kathleen had placed next to the turkey, and thrust into the perspiring bird.

Punctuating my assault on the steaming fowl with increasingly liberal swallows of vintage Scotch, I successfully finished off the job in fifteen or twenty minutes. While I sliced away, Don observed, grinning and guzzling.

The firemen completed their work just after I'd begun my own surgery. They declined Don's offer of a holiday libation—after all, there might be more walls to cut down that evening—and suggested that he tape plastic covers over the exposed portions of his livingroom wall in order to retain a modicum of warmth from the central heating system.

My duties done, I watched Kathleen and another woman scoop stuffing from the ravaged carcass while downing the few remaining drops from my tumbler. I looked over at Don, who offered me his right hand while holding the bottle in his left. We shook hands and I declined Kathleen's invitation to join them for dinner, explaining that I now had to perform the same service at my house.

Several of the guests were already patching plastic tarps onto the livingroom walls, and I waved to them on my way out. Everyone appeared to be having a good time. As I descended the front steps, I heard Kathleen shout, "Is anybody hungry?" followed by a collective roar of assent.

I felt a bit wobbly from the whiskey so decided, to leave my car parked on Don's street and walk home. Fortified as I was, the cold air refreshed me, and I made my way not unhappily under the black, starless sky, unbothered by the snowflakes caressing my head like they had Johnny McQueen's.

The Lost Christmas

In 1954, when I was eight years old, I lost Christmas. At about noon of Christmas Eve that year, I went with some kids to the Nortown Theater on Western Avenue in Chicago to see a movie Demetrius and the Gladiators, starring Victor Mature and Susan Hayward. My mother and I had until earlier that month been living in Florida and Cuba, and were in Chicago, where I was born and where we sometimes stayed, to spend the Christmas holidays with Nanny, my grandmother, my mother's mother, who was bed-ridden because of a chronic heart condition. In fact, Nanny would die due to heart failure the following May, at the age of fifty-nine.

The ground was piled with fresh snow that Christmas Eve Day. The few cars that were moving snailed along the streets barely faster than we could walk. The first time I had come to Chicago as a human being old enough to be conscious of my surroundings was when I was five or six. My mother was taking a trip to Mexico or Hawaii or Jamaica, some exotic place, it was the middle of February, and she decided to leave me for a couple of weeks with Nanny. The outside temperature rarely rose above zero during that visit. Coming from Key West and Miami, Florida, and Havana, Cuba, where I was used to wearing not much more than shorts and a T-shirt, I became convinced that I had been lied to: hell was not hot, it was freezing cold. A person did not have to wait until after death to go there, either; I had already arrived. I also believed that my mother must really hate me to leave me in such a terrible place. I couldn't even go out-side because the sidewalks were solid sheets of ice and all I did was fall whenever I tried to walk on them. When my mother returned from her holiday two weeks later, caramel-skinned from the sun, which I thought had burned out, she appeared to me like an alien being, an inhabitant of another galaxy who bore no relation to the Arctic outpost at which I'd been abandoned. Now that I was older, however, and was somewhat inured to the snow and ice—at least I knew what to expect—I could if not enjoy at least endure the weather, especially since I knew my sit-uation was temporary.

I thought Demetrius and the Gladiators was a great movie, full of fighting with swords and shields and a sexy redhead, like my mother. I didn't notice if Victor Mature's breasts were larger than Susan Hayward's—an earlier (1949) film, Samson and Delilah, had prompted the comment by a producer that Mature's tits were bigger than co-star Hedy Lamarr's—I was impressed only by the pageantry of goofy Hollywood ancient Rome. Walking home Christmas Eve afternoon, the leaden gray Chicago sky heading rapidly toward darkness, I suddenly was overcome by dizziness and very nearly collapsed to the now ice-hard sidewalk carapace. My companions had already turned off onto another street, so I was alone. I managed to steady myself against a brown brick wall and then slowly and carefully made my way the final block or two to my grandmother's house.

The next thing I knew I was waking up in bed dressed in my yellow flannel pajamas decorated with drawings of football players. The first image I saw was a large-jawed fullback cradling a ball in the crook of his left arm while stiff-arming a would-be tackler with his right. I was very thirsty and looked up to see my mother and Nanny, who, miraculously, was out of her sickbed, leaning over me. According to my mother, I asked two questions: "Can I have a glass of water?" and "Is it Christmas yet?"

In fact, it was December 26th—I had lost consciousness almost as soon as I arrived home following the movie, and had been delirious with fever for most of the time since then. The fever broke and I woke up. My mother brought me a glass of water, which she cautioned me to sip slowly, as the doctor had ordered.

"Was the doctor here?" I asked. Nanny and my mother told me how worried they had been. A doctor friend of Nanny's had come twice to see me, even on Christmas Day; he would come again later. Nanny and my mother laughed—in fact, both of them were crying tears of relief.

"This is the best gift of all," said my mother, "getting my boy back."

I've often wondered what I missed during my delirium, as if those twenty-four or so hours had been stolen from me. Once someone asked me if I had access to a time machine and could go forward or back anywhere in time, where would I go? I told him without hesitation that I would set the machine for Christmas Day of 1954. To paraphrase William Faulkner, that Christmas past is not dead, it's not even past.

The Winner

My mother and I spent Christmas and New Year's of 1957 in Chicago. By this time, being ten years old and having experienced portions of the northern winter on several occasions, I was prepared for the worst. On our way to Chicago on the long drive from Florida, I excitedly anticipated playing in deep snow and skating on icy ponds. It turned out to be a mild winter, however, very unusual for Chicago in that by Christmas Day there had been no snow.

"The first snowfall is always around Thanksgiving," said Pops, my grandfather. "This year, you didn't need a coat. It's been the longest Indian summer ever."

I didn't mind being able to play outside with the kids who lived on Pops's street, but I couldn't hide my disappointment in not seeing snow, something we certainly did not get in Key West. The neighborhood boys and girls were friendly enough, though I felt like an outsider, even though I'd known some of them from previous visits for as many as three years.

By New Year's Eve it still had not snowed and my mother and I were due to leave on the second of January. I complained to her about this and she said, "Baby, sometimes you just can't win."

I was invited on New Year's Day to the birthday party of a boy I didn't know very well, Jimmy Kelly, a policeman's son who lived in an apartment in a three-flat at the end of the block. Johnny and Billy Duffy, who lived next door to Pops, persuaded me to come with them. Johnny was my age, Billy one year younger; they were good pals of Kelly's and assured me Kelly and his parents wouldn't mind if I came along. Just to make sure, the Duffy brothers' mother called Jimmy Kelly's mother and she said they'd be happy to have me.

Since the invitation had come at practically the last minute and all of the toy stores were closed because of the holiday, I didn't have a proper present to bring for Jimmy Kelly. My mother put some candy in a bag, wrapped Christmas paper around it, tied on a red ribbon and handed it to me.

"This will be okay," she said. "Just be polite to his parents and thank them for inviting you."

"They didn't invite me," I told her, "Johnny and Billy did. Mrs. Duffy called Kelly's mother."

"Thank them anyway. Have a good time."

At Kelly's house, kids of all ages were running around, screaming and yelling, playing tag, knocking over lamps and tables, driving the family's two black cocker spaniels, Mick and Mack, crazy. The dogs were running with and being trampled by the marauding children. Officer Kelly, in uniform with his gunbelt on, sat in a chair by the front door drinking beer out of a brown bottle. He was a large man, overweight, almost bald. He didn't seem to be at all disturbed by the chaos.

Mrs. Kelly took my gift and the Duffy brothers' gift for Jimmy, said, "Thanks, boys, go on in," and disappeared into the kitchen.

Johnny and Billy and I got going with the others and after a while Mrs. Kelly appeared with a birthday cake and ice cream. The cake had twelve candles on it, eleven for Jimmy's age and one for good luck. Jimmy was a big fat kid and blew all of the candles out in one try with ease. We each ate a piece of chocolate cake with a scoop of vanilla ice cream, then Jimmy opened his gifts. He immediately swallowed most of the candy my mother had put into the bag.

Mrs. Kelly presided over the playing of several games, following each of which she presented the winner with a prize. I won most of these games, and with each successive victory I became increasingly embarrassed. Since I was essentially a stranger, not really a friend of the birthday boy's, the other kids, including Johnny and Billy Duffy, grew somewhat hostile toward me. I felt badly about this, and after winning a third or fourth game decided that was enough—even if I could win another game, I would lose on purpose so as not to further antagonize anyone else.

The next contest, however, was to be the last, and the winner was to receive the grand prize, a brand new professional model football autographed by Bobby Layne, quarterback of the champion Detroit Lions. Officer Kelly, Mrs. Kelly told us, had been given this ball personally by Bobby Layne, whom he had met while providing security for him when the Lions came to Chicago to play the Bears.

The final event was not a game but a raffle. Each child picked a small, folded piece of paper out of Officer Kelly's police hat. A number had been written on every piece of paper by Mrs. Kelly. Officer Kelly had already decided what the winning number would be and himself would announce it following the children's choices.

I took a number and waited, seated on the floor with the other kids, not even bothering to see what number I had chosen. Officer Kelly stood up, holding the football in one huge hand, and looked at the kids, each of whom, except for me, waited eagerly to hear the magic number which they were desperately hoping would be the one they had plucked out of the policeman's hat. Even Jimmy had taken a number.

"Sixteen," said Officer Kelly.

Several of the kids groaned loudly, and they all looked at one another to see who had won the football. None of them had it. Then their heads turned in my direction. There were fifteen other children at the party and all thirty of their eyes burned into mine. Officer and Mrs. Kelly joined them. I imagined Mick and Mack, the cocker spaniels, staring at me, too, their tongues hanging out, waiting to bite me should I admit to holding the precious number sixteen.

I unfolded my piece of paper and there it was: 16. I looked up directly into the empty pale green and yellow eyes of Officer Kelly. I handed him the little piece of paper and he scrutinized it, as if inspecting it for forgery. The kids looked at him, hoping against hope that there had been a mistake, that somehow nobody, especially me, had chosen the winning number.

Officer Kelly raised his eyes from the piece of paper and stared again at me.

"Your father is a Jew, isn't he?" Officer Kelly said.

I didn't answer. Officer Kelly turned to his wife and asked, "Didn't you tell me his old man is a Jew?"

"His mother's a Catholic," said Mrs. Kelly. "Her people are from County Kerry."

"I don't want the football," I said, and stood up. "Jimmy should have it, it's his birthday."

Jimmy got up and grabbed the ball out of his father's hand.

"Let's go play!" he shouted, and ran out the door.

The kids all ran out after him.

I looked at Mrs. Kelly. "Thanks," I said, and started to walk out of the apartment.

"You're forgetting your prizes," said Mrs. Kelly, "the toys you won."

"It's okay," I said.

"Happy New Year!" Mrs. Kelly shouted after me.

When I got home my mother asked if it had been a good party.

"I guess," I said.

She could tell there was something wrong but she didn't push me. That was one good thing about my mother, she knew when to leave me alone. It was getting dark and she went to draw the drapes.

"Oh, baby," she said, "come look out the window. It's snowing."

The Lonely
and the Lost
A NOVELLA

Dedicated to the memories
of Douglas Sirk and James Ross

the pharaoh's flame

A boy and girl, both in their late teens, clung desperately to the body of a giant Harley as it tore along an unpaved country road, his hands clamped to the preposterously raised handles of the cycle's sissy bars, hair and fringe flying, screaming, shouting over the roar of the huge engine, flying free. In the near distance, sparkling red and orange in the black electric night sky, they saw a sign: THE PHARAOH'S FLAME. The boy guided his streaking monster bike into a parking area and slid it to a stop among a motley collection of other motorcycles, pickup trucks and absurdly raked and otherwise zanily configured and constructed kit cars and mean lean vehicles. He cut his Harley's roar and they were instantly captivated by music pounding, thumping against the walls of the roadhouse, a maddening sound that drove the boy and girl crazy before they could enter the place. They ran up the steps and tore open the doors.

Now the music was much louder, and the motorcycle couple lost themselves in the gyrating crowd already abandoned to the cacophonous frenzy. The scene was a cross between Breughel's peasant wedding and the Ninth Circle of Dante's Hell, the music a mixture of blues and country rock raised to a new and altogether unearthly level. Anything went on this dance floor.

Up on the bandstand were several swaying, seriously sweating young beasts, seven in all, two of whom, both wielding guitars like carving knives, stood in front of the others. These two were in their late twenties, raw, handsome young men off whose faces and bodies liquid jumped as they seemingly bent their instruments, making them screech and howl, creating a caterwaul that increasingly incited the crowd before them to greater and greater heights of rapture and near hysteria. One of the guitarists scowled maniacally while the other's face was frozen in a beatific grin. This was Saturday night and the band was tearing down the building.

In the crowd a huge woman grabbed a man by his throat and choked him, holding him off the ground. A young girl pulled the large woman's hair and sank her sharp, tiny teeth into Brünhilde's shoulder, trying to get the rhinoceros-sized lady to release her stranglehold on the man, whom she outweighed by perhaps a hundred pounds. The musicians, as well as the other dancers, were oblivious to the trio struggling in their midst, ignoring them while locked in their own solipsistic trances.

Squirming her way through this jactitating battlefield, a

woman in her late twenties, very beautiful and better-dressed than anyone else in the place, fought her way toward the exit. A man followed her, worming a similar path. He was the same age as the woman but looked ten years older, his once seriously handsome face compromised by a broken nose and several knife-slash scars on either cheek. It was impossible to know whether she was fleeing and he was chasing her or if they were in concert in their movement. Finally the woman reached the front door and pushed her way out, escaping the din. She hurried down the front steps and walked quickly toward the parking area.

"Kiss! Wait! Come back!"

She ignored her pursuer's plea and continued walking.

"Forget it, Torch! Leave me be!"

The woman reached her car, a sleek, late-model beauty like herself, and opened the driver's side door, but before she could get in the man reached her and grabbed her by both shoulders.

"Damn it, Kiss, I'm sorry. I won't bring it up no more."

"Get this, Torch Martin. Just because you're fuckin' another man's wife doesn't mean she don't care for her husband!"

"Kismet, I..."

She looked hard, defiantly into the man's eyes, but her attitude softened significantly as she spoke. It was impossible for her to disguise her deep feeling for him.

"You always was hot shit around here, Torch. But bein' a high school football star and local stud don't go very far in the real world, does it? You can't pick on Monty now like you could when we were kids. You need me to shake him down. Well, I won't do it, I won't. I ain't so cockstruck by you I'd set up my own husband for a fall."

"Look, Kiss, I told you to forget I ever said anything. I'll figure out some other way to get the money. I'm just a little desperate now, is all."

He went to kiss her but Kismet turned her head away.

"You gonna let me get in my car or you gonna knock me around? Nobody gonna say nothin', they see you do it. Not in front of your own place, anyway."

Torch let go of her.

"Go on, Kiss. Run on back to Mr. Rhodes and his daddy's dollars."

The roadhouse door banged open and exploding out of it came two gigantic, shitkicking monsters, locked in mutual deathgrips. They rolled around in the dirt, tearing and clubbing at one another until two men emerged from the building wielding blackjacks. The men set upon the scuffling pair until the fighters were bloodied and still.

One of the security men, breathing hard, looked over and saw Torch standing with Kismet.

"What should we do with 'em, boss?"

"Move 'em out of the way, Ralphie. Just drag their fat carcasses to the side so people don't trip over 'em. Then you and Dogeyes get back inside, see things don't get too much more out of control."

Ralphie and Dogeyes followed orders and Torch returned his

attention to Kismet. He opened her car door, allowing her to slip behind the wheel.

"I'll talk to you later, honey. I'm sorry. Things has just been damn difficult for me lately."

Kismet leaned toward him and kissed Torch softly on the lips.

"I know, baby."

She closed her door, started up the car and drove away.

a star fell from heaven

The next afternoon, Jack and Jesse McDonald, the guitarists who had led the band the night before, were seated together at a table inside The Pharaoh's Flame. Jack, the scowler, held his right index finger under a line in a book opened on the table from which he read aloud. As Jack read slowly, Jesse mumbled incomprehensibly along with him.

"What was Madame de Bargeton beside that angel radiant with youth, hope, and the future," Jack read, "with her wonderful smile, her great dark eyes that seemed as deep as the sky, as brilliant as the sun?"

Jesse nodded and moved his lips, smiling and excited. He spoke to Jack in a language only his brother could understand, then motioned with one hand for Jack to continue.

"She was smiling and chatting with Madame Firmiani, one of the most charming women in Paris. A voice in him said: 'Intellect is the lever with which a man can move the world.' But another voice replied that money is the fulcrum of intellect."

"That ain't no lie, boys."

Jack and Jesse looked up to see Torch Martin standing in front of them.

Jack's scowl held as he said, "Hello, Torch. You're up early today." Then he noticed Kismet walking up behind Torch and something approaching a smile crossed his face. "Hello, Kiss," he said.

Jesse's ever-present grin widened considerably at the sight of Kismet Rhodes. He pointed at the book and then at her. Kismet went over to Jesse and ran a hand through his hair, showing her obvious, sisterly affection for him.

"What are you reading, Jack?" she asked.

"*Lost Illusions* by Honoré de Balzac, a Frenchman. He's probably dead by now, but he wrote lots of books. This one's Jesse's favorite."

Jesse spoke to Kismet in his special language and she laughed.

"I ain't no angel, Jesse," she said, "really I ain't. Just ask Torch here."

"You understand Jess pretty well, Kiss," said Jack. "I'm amazed."

"All a person has to do is listen. Not many'll take the time, listen to anybody else."

"It sure makes him happy. Hey, when you gonna come back and sing with us?"

"Yeah, Kiss," said Torch. "Or ain't singin' in a roadhouse proper behavior for the wife of Little Egypt, Mississippi's leading citizen?"

Kismet shot Torch a dirty look.

"Okay, okay, baby!" he said, backing away from her, his hands up. "I was just kiddin'."

Dogeyes came in, accompanied by a portly, balding, well-dressed middle-aged man.

"Torch," said Dogeyes, "Mr. Host here says he got to talk to you."

The portly man curled his upper lip, which was his version of a smile, and said, "Afternoon, Mrs. Rhodes. Saw your convertible out front. Hello, Torch."

"Dogeyes, take Hubert here into my office," Torch said. "Then move Mrs. Rhodes's car around back. The keys are in it."

Dogeyes blinked rapidly several times and nodded. "Sure thing."

"I'll be right in, Hubert."

Hubert Host nodded heavily toward Kismet, extruding his double dewlap, and left with Dogeyes.

Torch took Kismet's left hand in his own.

"You be all right with the boys while I do some business, honey, won't you?"

Kismet laughed and said, "Since when did you start worryin' so much about me, Torch? Not that I don't appreciate the thought."

Torch lifted her hand to his lips and kissed it.

"Like Bert Gordon, the gambler, said to Fast Eddie in The Hustler, after Eddie asked him, 'When did you adopt me?' I'm not sure just when it was."

Torch released Kismet's hand and walked toward his office.

"Seriously, Kiss," said Jack, "Jesse and I would really dig it if you'd start singin' again."

"Tell you what, Jack, you know that home for the mentally impaired up at Oriental, where my mama died?"

"Sure, it's where they wanted to send Jesse when he was a kid, only our folks wouldn't allow it."

"Well, I got Monty on the executive board now. They got a singin' group made up of patients, and they're comin' to Little Egypt to do a benefit performance for the Institute. I talked Torch into lettin' 'em stage it here at The Pharaoh's Flame. I'd like you and Jesse and the band to play with 'em."

"And you'll sing with us?"

Kismet smiled. "I'll sing with you."

Jesse picked up a guitar, an acoustic flat-top, and motioned for his brother to do the same. The boys began to pick out a familiar tune, "A Star Fell from Heaven," a song made popular by Bill Monroe, knowing Kismet could not resist singing it. As she did, Ralphie, Dogeyes and Mudcat, a young kid who did odd jobs around the Flame, came in, pulled up chairs and sat down and listened.

Torch Martin sat in his office across his desk from Hubert Host.

"It's an old song, Hubert, but you know I'm good for it."

"Torch, I known you since you was born, practically. Your daddy, old Tommy, and me come up together, went to the goddamn war together."

Torch snorted. "Hubert, spare me this corny shit. I got me

some serious gamblin' debts, that's all. I already put the Flame on the line and I'm expectin' some funds to come in on an outside investment any day now. That'll do to more'n pay off Al Ball. Tell Mr. Ball he'll have his money next week. Tommy Martin never welshed on a debt and neither has his son. That's about all I got to tell you, Hubert, now get out."

Hubert Host stood up a bit unsteadily.

"You'd do well to behave better by me, Torch. I'm an old family friend."

He smacked his lips together, brushing them with a dry tongue.

"Ain't you even gonna offer me a drink?" Hubert asked. Then he emitted a loud fart.

Torch stood up, came around the desk and took hold of Hubert by the lapels of his jacket.

"You're a mess, Hubert, you know that? Bein' an ugly, flatulent drunk is one thing, but bein' a faggot's another. I know all about you and your girlfriend Webb Wirt. Daddy told me to stay away from you when I was a boy. Said, don't let ol' Hubert put his hands where you can't see 'em. You sick fuck!"

Torch pushed Hubert away from him. The fat man staggered but righted himself by grabbing on to the back of the chair in which he'd been sitting.

"You're sick, too, Torch!" He said, his pink eyes reddening further as the blood rose in his head. "You're sick just like me, like Al Ball, like most everybody you ever gonna meet! You had a chance once, oh yeah, but you fucked up. Your old daddy made sure of it, teachin' his kid how to burn down buildings. Hell, yes, you got the sickness in you. It's all over your cut up face. As the Lord saith to Jeremiah, 'Will ye steal, murder, and commit adultery, and swear falsely, and burn incense unto Ba'al, and walk after other gods whom ye know not…. And I will cast you out of my sight…'"

Torch made a sudden move, as if to go after Hubert.

"I'm gonna cast you out, you old fool!"

Hubert turned, wobbled, then half-ran out of Torch's office. He kept going and passed the others without saying goodbye.

"Mudcat!" Torch shouted, as he came out front. "Bring Mrs. Rhodes' car around for her."

"Right now," said Mudcat, and he dashed outside.

"Am I goin' somewhere?" Kismet asked.

Torch calmed down at the sight of her.

"I've got something to take care of, Kiss, and I need Jack and Jesse to help me."

Jack stood up and said, "Kiss is gonna sing with us, Torch. When the Oriental folks come to town."

"I'd almost forgotten about that."

Kismet kissed him on the cheek. "I won't let you forget, darlin'."

Torch grinned. "I don't guess you will."

secrets in the dark

Torch Martin had the pedal to the metal of his cherried-out 1978 Oldsmobile Cutlass. Jack McDonald rode shotgun and Jesse was in the back seat as Torch rodded his midnight blue short along an unlit two-lane, the Cutlass's brights searing the semi-darkness like laser beams. Torch took a long swig from a pint of Old Overholt and handed the bottle to Jack.

"Webb Wirt was a doctor once," said Martin, "in some town in South Carolina, I think. He got caught sellin' morphine and done some hard time. After that, he hooked up with Hubert Host and they both went to work for Al Ball, pushin' booze, drugs, slot machines, girls. Webb was slicker'n his squeeze, Hubert, though. Built him up his own tidy fortune based on cheap rental houses in small cities all over the state of Mississippi. Man supposed to still possess the first cent he ever made. Keeps to himself up on Picnic Hill. Hubert's about his only visitor, I hear."

Jack swallowed a little rye and passed the bottle back to Torch. He knew his brother wouldn't want any.

"We're goin' to Webb Wirt's house?" asked Jack.

"Just gonna look the place over. See what we can see."

Torch whipped his car around every curve without slowing down at all, as if the Cutlass were the only vehicle on the road that night. Jack prayed it was.

"Look, Torch, I told you I wasn't gonna be in on none of these deals anymore. I got a future with the music. Me and Jesse got plans."

"Sheriff finds out about some of your past activities, Jack, what you think'll become of your brother? I mean with you bein' in the pen."

"You'd be in there with me."

"Prob'ly would, yeah. But Jesse don't depend on me for much."

Torch killed the pint and tossed the empty bottle out his window.

Jesse started talking, gesticulating wildly, pounding his hands on the back of Jack's seat. Jack turned around and looked at him.

"I hear you, brother," Jack said.

Jesse stopped talking, sat back in his seat, and smiled at him. Heavy raindrops began to pelt the car.

As he drove, Torch thought about Kismet, who at that moment was at home, stripping off her clothes. Only one small lamp was on in her bedroom and when a flash of lightning suddenly illuminated the house, Kismet was startled. She headed for her bathroom but stopped when a figure appeared in the doorway. Another flash of electricity lit the room, revealing Kismet's husband, Monty. He was entirely naked and holding a large sword.

Torch, Jack and Jesse crept up Picnic Hill in the rain. When they got to the house, they split up, as Torch had instructed before leaving the car, in order to spy on different parts of Webb Wirt's domicile. The ground was becoming increasingly mushy as the rain soaked in, and the men began to slide and slip. Torch and Jack circled the house from opposite directions, seeing nothing through the windows, no movement, no glimpse of Webb Wirt, only darkness.

When Torch and Jack met, Torch said, "Where's that idiot brother of yours?"

"He ain't an idiot. Don't call him an idiot."

"Idiot or not, where the hell has he got to?"

The two men sat on their haunches in the rain, looking around. Then they heard a kind of murmur, followed by a babbling noise.

"There he is," said Jack, pointing down the side of the house.

Torch looked and saw one of Jesse's hands waving at them from a basement window, motioning for Torch and Jack to come over.

"Let's go," Jack said. "He's inside."

The two men crawled through the window and found themselves in the basement with Jesse. Torch fired his Zippo and waved it around. The basement was filled with all kinds of junk, including statuary; large, ornately framed paintings; boxes overflowing with old clothes; stand-up fans; bedsprings; and stacks and stacks of magazines and books.

"God damn," said Torch, "it stinks in here. Hot, too."

"Yeah, there is a weird odor, all right."

Jesse began to wend his way through the maze, signalling for Jack and Torch to follow.

"Where's he think he's goin'?" asked Torch.

A shaft of light filtered into the basement from a crack in the ceiling, and directly under it was a large safe, five-and-a-half feet high and three feet wide; an old key and combination Herring-Hall-Marvin made in Hamilton, Ohio, in the 1920s. Jesse grinned widely as he showed it to Torch and Jack.

Jack smiled, too, and said, "I told you he wasn't no idiot."

Torch put away his lighter and ran his hands over the outside of the safe.

"The stuff that dreams are made of," he said.

"What?"

"What's inside this baby. This here's our black bird."

"Now who's talkin' crazy?"

A sliding noise froze the three men. There was a sound like the rustling of papers or leaves, only more protracted. Jesse started humming and pointed to the ceiling. Torch and Jack looked up and saw a huge, coffee-colored python lying on the crossbeam above them.

"Okay, boys," said Torch, "let's move slowly back toward where we come in."

The three men retraced their steps, trying not to make any noise. They climbed back out the window, Jack making sure it was shut tightly behind them, before running like hell through the rain to Torch's car.

ruler of my heart

Torch was driving alone on an empty road, lights off at four A.M., Irma Thomas's "Ruler of My Heart" blasting as loud as the speakers would bear. An empty short dog rattled around on the floor and Torch tromped it with his left foot. He punched up a number on his car phone.

"Kiss! Kiss! It's me!" he spat into it, then turned down the music. "I gotta see you."

"Where are you?" Kismet whispered to him.

"Halfway to hell, I guess."

"Where are you?"

"I'll be up by Ringtail Lake in five minutes. Meet me there."

Torch hung up and pumped the volume back to maximum. The Cutlass shimmied as Torch punished the accelerator.

The sky had cleared and Torch sat on the hood of his Olds sipping from a fresh half-pint when Kismet's Mercedes pulled up next to him. Irma Thomas was singing "Time Is On My Side" as Kismet got out and Torch jumped down to greet her. He set the bottle on the Mercedes' hood, took Kismet in his arms and they danced. Stars fell on Ringtail Lake.

"What am I gonna do about you?" said Kismet. "This is crazy."

"You went for the money, baby. I don't blame you. I'm just glad you got the good sense not to ignore your real feelings."

"Mama's goin' insane pushed me to it, Torch. You know that. What if it happens to me?"

"No problem. If Rhodes don't want you around no more, I'll lock you up in one of the cabins behind the Flame, feed you and fuck you. You won't be hurtin'."

"Oh, Torch, stop. I'm not kiddin'."

"I wouldn't let you down, Kiss. Not after all these years we been doin' good for each other."

Torch whirled her around, then stopped and kissed her hard. They sank slowly to the wet grass. Kismet pulled Torch's shirt out of his pants and reached for his belt buckle. They had been lovers since they were teenagers, and each knew what the other liked and needed. No matter what else happened, they discovered, their mutual physical response was always completely honest and immediate. Making love was the only pure time either of them had, the only time that they were without guile and were entirely unburdened.

A short distance away, crouched down by the shore of the lake, Monty Rhodes watched.

Inside Al Ball's office, it was impossible to know whether it was day or night. The shades were always drawn and only a dim light permitted limited discernment of the features of whomever was in the room. On this occasion, Hubert Host and Ralphie sat abreast in chairs on one side of a large oak desk. Al Ball, a tall, completely hairless man with severe skin problems, sat in a high-backed wicker chair on the other side. His face was covered with sores that wept copiously, causing him to pat continually at his ooze with a handkerchief.

"So, Hubert," said Al Ball, "what about it? Is Martin gonna come up with the dough?"

"He says next week, but..."

"But you think he's stallin'."

"Maybe he's got an idea."

Ball grunted. "What's the scam on The Pharaoh's Flame, Ralphie? How deep is Torch in hock?"

"Up to his ears, Mr. Ball."

"Um, um."

Ralphie found it difficult to keep his eyes on Al Ball's face, despite the low wattage. Ball pressed a blue cotton hanky to his right cheek, held it there for several seconds, then removed and looked at it.

"What if we turned his daddy's game on him?" he said. "What if we burned the place? He insured?"

"Maybe," said Ralphie. "People's prob'ly think he done it himself."

Al Ball laughed. "There you go. Hubert, check it out."

"Yes, Al."

Ball stood up and walked around the desk and stopped next to Ralphie. Al towered over him and stared down at the top of Ralphie's head, weaving a bit from side to side. Ball allowed the liquid from his face to drip onto Ralphie, forming spots on the collar and shoulders of the seated man's shirt. Ralphie did not move, however, letting the secretions stain his clothing.

"Ralphie, you work for Torch Martin."

"I do, Mr. Ball."

"Martin trusts you?"

"I suppose so."

"But you been a grass for Hubert here."

"Uh...a grass?"

"Yeah, a snitch. You feed him dope."

"He pays me for information."

"Who do you suppose pays Hubert, Ralphie?"

"You do, I guess, Mr. Ball."

"I do, Ralphie. I pay Hubert, and I pay everybody else in this room."

Al's face began to drip even more furiously. He wiped it with the blue hanky, soaking it. He let the handkerchief drop to the floor.

"Edgar!" he said to one of his henchmen who stood by the door. "Get me some tissues."

Edgar took a packet of Kleenex from one of his pockets, brought it to his boss, then resumed his position by the door.

Ball mopped his cheeks with the tissues.

"I have to tell ya, Ralphie, I got a problem with snitches. I gotta use 'em sometimes, but it don't mean I like 'em. I figure, if Torch Martin got an employee such as you, who, I would suppose he trusts, as you say, or else why are you there workin' for him in the first place, right? Right?"

"Right," said Ralphie.

"Now, indirectly or not, I pay you. I mean, it's Hubert, maybe, or Edgar, or Goofy the fuckin' dog gives you the money in your hand, but you understand the source whereof it comes, yes? Yes?"

"Sure, yes. From you, Mr. Ball."

"Mr. Ball, right. Right you are, Ralphie, doll. I am definitely him. Mr. Ball. Himself. Now, Ralphie, you keep up Hubert here on Mr. Martin's situation. You tell him who comes and goes there, at The Pharaoh's Flame, how many times a day he bangs the Rhodes dame, what the take is on a weekend from the crowd comes to hear that hideous noise."

Al Ball walked away from Ralphie, patting down his face.

"I tell you what kind of music I like," he said. "Ethel Merman singing 'There's No Business Like Show Business.' You know that, Ralphie?"

"No, Mr. Ball, sir, I don't."

"Well, this will be a special day for you, my boy, a very special day."

Al Ball pushed a button on a CD player and Ethel Merman's voice burst into the room. As the speakers blared "There's No Business Like Show Business," Al Ball sang along with her, imitating Ethel Merman's Broadway gestures, holding wads of tissue in each hand with his arms spread wide. The other men in the room had no choice but to sit and listen as Al Ball and Ethel Merman unleashed their ungodly serenade.

the chosen few

Jack and Jesse sat on the short porch of the cabin in which they lived behind The Pharaoh's Flame. It was a sunny, balmy early afternoon, the kind of day where all seemed right with the world even though almost nothing was. The McDonald brothers were working out guitar parts for some new songs.

A dusty, banged-up, several-year-old Plymouth sedan made its way up the road toward the boys' cabin and shuddered to a stop in front of it. A man slowly emerged from behind the steering wheel and walked toward them. He was paunchy, in early middle-age, dressed in a shabby brown sport coat and shiny black slacks. His hair was crew-cut and his face was clean-

shaven and red. Halfway up the path to the cabin it was clear
that he was almost out of breath. He stopped and lit a cigaret,
started to pull a flask from one of his coat pockets, then thought
better of it and continued up to the porch, put one foot on the
first step and stopped.

"Hello, fellas," he said, "my name's Billy Breaux. You maybe
heard of my record label, Strange Cajun? I'm da man discovered
Tick-Tock Wheatstraw, Bitty Royce, Alphonse 'Froo Froo'
Desjardins. You know, 'Don't Touch My Toucan If I Can't Touch
Yours.' Froo Froo hit top da charts wit dat."

Jack leaned forward in his chair and extended his right hand.

"I'm Jack. This is Jesse."

The two men shook. Billy Breaux then extended his hand to
Jesse, but Jesse just grinned at the man. Billy grinned back.

"I come all da way up from New Orleans to hear you guys.
Got an arrangement wid a sound studio in Nashville. We could
make some noise there, y'all feel like it."

Jesse mumbled a blue streak to Jack. When he quit, Billy
asked, "Did y'all ever do any recordin'?"

"No, sir," said Jack. "That Froo Froo and Tick-Tock and them,
must be fifteen years ago they was on top. You don't mind my
askin', what you been up to lately?"

Billy Breaux took a long drag on his cigaret, then dropped the
butt in the dust at his feet and killed it with his toe.

"I ain't a liar, Jack, I tell you straight. Had some troubles, son,
landed me in the state penitentiary at Parchman. This music bid-

ness can try your soul, you allow it. I was a bad actor there for a bit, I admit. Bad drugs, bad women, bad decisions. Every day got to be bad day at Black Rock for me. Cost me a baker's dozen years of my life."

Billy wiped sweat from his forehead with a jacket sleeve, felt for his flask again but left it in the pocket.

"You can take a pull you need one, Mr. Breaux. Okay by us."

Billy smiled. "Sometimes I have the shakes, is what it is, Jack. Never did have the shakes until I was inside."

"Thirteen years is a long time."

"Got caught with another man's wife and beat him to death with his own pistol. Ripley, Mississippi. Hell, it was self-defense but they give me manslaughter. Now I'm workin' my way back onliest way I know how, discoverin' new talent, of which my grapevine inform me you boys got plenty."

"'Preciate your comin' to hear us, Mr. Breaux. Jesse'n I'll be playin' our asses off tonight, startin' around nine."

Billy shook Jack's hand again and smiled at Jesse, who nodded and grinned at the man.

"I'll be here," said Billy. "Been a pleasure meetin' you gentlemen."

Jack and Jesse watched Billy Breaux make his way back to his car. Billy coughed heavily and had to rest against the automobile before getting in. He waved out the window at the brothers as he drove off, and they waved back.

Mudcat came walking out of the dust kicked up by Billy's departure.

"Hey, Jack. Whassup?"

"Not too much, Cat. Me an' Jesse's just figurin' out a few things. Yourself?"

Mudcat sat down on the lowest porchstep. Jesse reached down and slapped hands with him, grinning brightly.

"Whassup, Jess?"

Jesse leaned back in his chair and ripped off a dazzling run on his guitar.

"Yow!" said Mudcat, who pulled out a harmonica from his pocket and began to play a chase, goading Jesse into a duet.

After several choruses, Mudcat quit, and said to Jack, "I'm supposed to tell you go see Torch. He's in his office."

Mudcat then resumed jamming with Jesse. Jack laid down his guitar, jumped down from the porch and strolled toward The Pharaoh's Flame. He noticed a police car parked in front.

In Torch's office, Sheriff Elihu Pitts sat in a chair counting some bills that were in an envelope. Satisfied that the amount was correct, the sheriff stuffed them back into the envelope, stood up and slid the envelope into his shirt. Sheriff Pitts was six-four and weighed about two hundred-seventy pounds. He was proud of his girth, and stuck his stomach out exaggeratedly as he spoke.

"I 'preciate this, Torch. Specially with the election comin' up."

"Sheriff, you know my respect for the law is profound," said Torch, punctuating his words with a shit-eating grin. "I don't know what us local businessmen would do without it."

"It makes me warm to hear you say this, Torch. A man like

me goes along, doin' his job, layin' his sore ass on the line for ord'nary citizens so's they can sleep in their beds nights solid as tree stumps. There's a certain about undescribable satisfaction in knowin' this, knowin' I'm doin' more'n my share. But sometimes, goddamit, Torch, I just gotta hear the words."

Torch nodded and said, "Fuck you, Pitts."

There was a knock at the door.

"Yeah?" said Torch.

The door opened and Jack stuck his head in.

"Mudcat said you wanted to see me."

"Come in, Jack."

Jack shut the door behind him.

"Afternoon, Jack," said Sheriff Pitts. "How's your idiot brother?"

Jack scowled. "Jesse's just fine, Sheriff."

"I hear you boys are quite the musicians. I'll have to come around soon and hear you play."

"That'd be our pleasure."

"Sure it would, Jack. I'm sure it would," Pitts said. "Well, men, I'd love to spend the day in idle chatter, but sure as my first wife Deltha had a purple birthmark size of a half-dollar on her portside buttock, there's bound to be some mothergrabbin' criminal drawin' down on an innocent person in some dark corner of Palestine County I'd better get to, drill the devil before he does serious harm. More mothergrabbers per square mile of Palestine County than even you two exceptionally perceptive individuals can imagine."

"You're in our prayers, Pitts," said Torch.

"Bless you, Mr. Martin. You take good care, now. You, too, Jack."

The sheriff walked out of the office with a grim expression on his face.

"Sit down, Jack," Torch said. "We got to talk about this Webb Wirt deal."

Jack remained standing.

"Damn it, Jack. Sit down!"

Jack sat down.

"You know me and Jesse don't want no part of it," he said.

"You ain't got a choice. I need you boys. Look, Jack, we ain't gonna kill him unless it's absolutely necessary."

"What about the snake?"

Torch waved his right hand dismissively. "That snake's full of rats, mice it catches. It don't aim to mess with us. If it bothers you, I'll plug it. Now, here's what's happenin'. We're goin' out to Webb Wirt's house after your last set tonight."

Jack stood up. "Like you say, I ain't got much of a choice."

Torch smiled. "For many be called, but few chosen. See you later, Jack."

a classical education

Jack drove into Little Egypt and parked his pickup truck on Main Street. He went into Palestine Hardware & Farm Supply and waved to a clerk.

"Hey, Rex. How you doin'?"

"Keepin' on keepin' on, Jack. Whenever life seems over-whelmin', I just consider the alternative. You lookin' for Puma?"

"I am."

"She's around back, in the pipeyard."

"Thanks much, Rex."

"You bet."

Jack walked through the length of the store and out a rear door into the yard. Long racks of uncut pipe were strategically arranged, along with stacks of fencing materials, barbed wire and fence posts. Jack spotted Puma, a slender, fair-haired woman of twenty. She was working with a length of pipe on a wooden horse, threading an end. Jack stopped a few yards away and smiled as she forced the threader around the one-and-a-half inch pipe, sweating and grunting. Her sleeves were rolled up, revealing serious muscles.

"I hate to stand by while a woman works," said Jack.

Puma did not look at him. She said, "Have a seat, then. You're an entertainer, entertain me."

"I didn't bring my guitar."

"Pity," she said, straining to make the cut, "I could stand to hear some tunes about now. What time is it, anyway?"

"Not sure. After two, I guess."

Puma stopped and looked at him. "Damn! I'm only supposed to work until one-thirty on Saturday. Nobody come out to stop me." She gave Jack a big smile. "Jesus, Jack McDonald, you're a goodlookin' fella. A dumb girl could fall for you."

Jack walked over, embraced Puma and kissed her on the fore-head, then on her lips. "I don't know any dumb girls," he said.

"I'm glad you come, Jack. I'm glad to see you. Can you give me a ride out to home? Mama's car died, so I let her take mine after she dropped me off this mornin'."

"No problem. How's your daddy?"

"Doc says he don't have much longer. Two, three weeks the most. It ain't horrible, though, like it could be. Least he don't seem to be in so much pain anymore. Just lies still, not talkin'. I sit with him and every once in a while he'll squeeze my hand and smile some."

Jack and Puma held hands and walked out of the pipeyard into the store.

"You owe me for a extra half-hour, Rex!" she shouted. "Mark it down!"

Rex nodded and grinned at her while he took care of a cus-tomer, giving Jack a quick wave.

Outside, Puma and Jack climbed into his truck, which he started up and drove away.

"So what's your news?" she asked, rolling down the passen-ger side window and letting the breeze hit her full in the face. "I'm hopin' to make it to the Flame tonight, if you're playin'."

"Yeah, we're playin'. Man come to see me and Jesse earlier. Record producer from New Orleans named Billy Breaux, had him some hot acts back in the days."

"Jack, that's great!"

"I guess."

"Somethin's botherin' you. Want to tell me?"

"No, Poo, I'm fine. Really." Jack did his best to supress a scowl. "Nothin's wrong. This Breaux fella's gonna be there tonight, too. You talk to him, see if you think he's for real. You got the best shit detector I come across."

Puma slid over and put her arms around Jack's neck, kissed his right cheek and snuggled her head into his shoulder.

"You're a good man, Jack, and I'm a damn good woman. If you had any brains you'd ask me to marry you. Our children would do some good in the world."

"I ain't arguin'."

"Jack, stop!" she said, sitting up straight.

By the side of the road was an old man with a long beard and a pack on his back, trudging along in the same direction Jack was driving. The man was carrying a large, aluminum bucket.

Jack pulled over and stopped the truck. The old man walked up to the passenger side window and stared at Puma. He was a mess, toothless, filth encrusted, but with clear eyes. He looked at Jack.

"You need a ride, mister?" Jack asked. "We're goin' up here about four miles. I can drop you at the junction."

"I am Idas," said the man in a high, thin voice, "son of Aphareus and brother of Lynceus. Once, I was considered the strongest of men. I challenged Apollo for Marpessa, my bride, after he had carried her off. It was Zeus himself who intervened and bade her choose; it was I she named.

"Thereafter, I sailed with the Argonauts, shipmate to the Dioscuri. When those sons of Zeus kidnapped Phoebe and Hilaeira, my brother and I pursued them. I slew Castor but Polydeuces slew Lynceus. I, also, was left for dead, but was rescued by wood-nymphs." He looked around keenly, narrowing his eyes to slits. "They protect me still. Hear their chatter?"

The old man raised his pail to the window. "Have you something for them? They are never far away."

Jack dug in his pocket and came up with a couple of dollar bills, which he passed to Puma, who put them into the bucket. The old man turned and trudged into the woods by the side of the road. The couple watched him until he had disappeared.

a better world than this

It was just past nine o'clock at night and a crowd had gathered outside The Pharaoh's Flame. People were talking and laughing, fooling around, listening to the music issuing forth from inside the roadhouse. Into the midst of the crowd came six large blonde young women riding loud motorcycles. The female riders braked to a stop near the roadhouse door, sat on their bikes and let them rumble as they straddled them. Each of the young women was wearing a black leather jacket with the words NOTHING BUT TRÜBL written on the back in white letters outlined by silver studs. They were the Trübl sisters: Tracy, Trina, Teresa, Taffy, Trudy and Tanya. Their first names were scripted on the left breast of their jackets. The Trübl sextuplets were the true

Amazons of Palestine County, Mississippi, and the crowd stood back from them, properly in awe.

Puma came zooming into the parking area in her car, a beat-up gray Dodge. She hopped out and headed for the music, greeting people as she went. As she passed the Trübls, with whom she had grown up and gone to school, she slapped hands with all six of them, while they were still astride their hogs.

"You girls are lookin' nasty!" Puma shouted, and the Trübls laughed. Then Puma entered the Flame.

A band had just finished their set and Puma pushed her way toward the stage. Torch Martin walked up to the microphone.

"Evenin', sinners!" he yelled. "Welcome to The Pharaoh's Flame. Y'all gonna get your heads bent tonight, that's certain. One way or the other!"

The crowd responded to Torch's promise with whistles and hollers.

"I got one for ya," he said. "Where do blondes go in the mornin'?" He paused for a moment before saying, "Home!"

Trudy Trübl, who with her five sisters was now standing in the back, screamed out, "Hey, Torch! Fuck you!"

Torch laughed. "See me later, kitten! Okay, folks, I ain't gonna keep y'all waitin' any longer, though I know, I just know, there are them among you that do appreciate a fella with a sense of humor."

Trina Trübl shouted, "Man with a dick your size best have a sense of humor!"

"What all got into you people tonight?" said Torch. "Whoa! O ye Egyptians and fellow wayfarers, our mouth is open unto you. Our heart is enlarged. The Pharaoh's Flame is honored as always to present Jack and Jesse and the Flamin' Band!"

Jack and Jesse and the boys kicked it to the top and the crowd went wild. Jack spotted Puma standing next to Billy Breaux in front of the stage and closed his eyes.

Seated in a booth in a dimly-lit restaurant in Little Egypt were Al Ball, Sheriff Pitts, Hubert Host and Al's henchman, Edgar. As always, Al continually wiped at his face with a cloth. A waitress brought drinks and set them in front of the men, taking away empty glasses.

"Sheriff," said Al, "it may surprise you to know that I am a reflective man. I reflect on things, I meditate on them. All manner of things, questions, situations. I wonder, I ponder. Each day when I awake I repeat to myself Hagakure's admonition: 'Die in your thoughts every morning and you will no longer fear death.'"

Pitts gulped at his glass, swallowed, then said, "Whatever gets you through, Mr. Ball, that's what you do."

Al grunted. "A human being is a despicable creature, really. Don't you think so, Sheriff? A human being will do anything to survive, to save himself. This is not an attitude to be admired, not in my opinion."

"Depends on the circumstance, wouldn't ya say?" the sheriff answered. "I mean, I once had a wild pig charge me and my old dog, Chester, a springer. Was in the woods out back of Rhodes

Refinery. Damn pig come out of nowhere. Kicked Chester to him, give me time to pull up my weapon. Shot the big bastard through the throat, but Chester was ground up about as bad as it gets. He been a good old doggie, too."

Al Ball wiped and nodded. He lifted his glass and stuck his green tongue in it and slurped at the contents.

"Sheriff," he said, "I want you to know that it's men such as yourself who hasten the extinction of our race. It would have been a far better thing had that swine torn into you than poor Chester. Of course, this is an expression of the long view. People spend their lives saving everything they can think of: animals, other people, trees, lakes. Entire communities nullified by newts, snail darters, spotted owls, lizard eels. I, for one, am looking forward, yes, forward, Sheriff Pitts, to the final fire, when this scurrilous civilization—so-called civilization—beckons the big cough drop to fall on itself and wipe out all this misery. You and your wild pig and dog. Chester, was it?"

"He said the name," said Hubert. "Chester."

"Thank you, Hubert," Ball said. "Which, come to think on it, would not be a bad name for a dog, or even a pig. Hubert, that is."

Al held up his glass. "Have another snort, Hubert."

Edgar laughed. "Snort, yeah, I get it."

"Pitts," said Al, allowing his face to drip onto the table and into his glass, "if you want to stay alive, you'd better go now. Just go. Don't delay. Don't offer any niceties. Remember the bald eagle that is the symbol of our nation's attitude. A vicious, evil bird whose wings beat terrifically inside our heads, batter with their razor-sharp talons at our terrified brains. Go on, sheriff, do not tarry from your appointed rounds."

Sheriff Pitts put down his glass, stood and seemed about to say something, then thought better of it and left the restaurant.

"Edgar, Hubert, the sheriff has an inadequate sense of humor." Al Ball resumed patting his face. "Certainly inadequate for my purposes. We will begin interviewing a potential replacement shortly, I assure you."

A waitress arrived carrying a large tray laden with plates. She proceeded to serve the three men gigantic steak dinners with mounds of mashed potatoes, heaps of vegetables, big bermuda onions and attendant condiments.

"Feedin' time, gentlemen," she announced.

"Nadine," said Al, "there is about you a delicacy that I find irresistible."

"Why, thank you, Mr. Ball. Comin' from a delicate type such as yourself makes all the difference in a remark like that."

"Nadine, have you ever had any ambition in the area of law enforcement?"

"Hell, no," she laughed. "I couldn't force nobody to do nothin'."

Al Ball sighed loudly. "A pity. The world would be a better place were it run by waitresses."

The men began to eat.

Monty Rhodes, dressed in a tuxedo, sat on the edge of a bed

in a hotel room in Birmingham, Alabama, holding a telephone to his left ear.

"Yes, operator," he said, "try that number again for me, please. Yes, I'll wait on the line."

Monty cradled the receiver between his ear and left shoulder and lit a cigaret. He puffed on it twice before a voice came on the other end.

"Hello?" said Kismet.

"Darling, darling," Monty said, spitting out the cigaret onto the carpet, "I've been trying to get through but the line's been busy for an hour. Who were you talking to?"

"Monty, that's so strange. Nobody. I haven't even been on the phone. There must have been some problem with the connection. Is it stormy in Birmingham? I know there's lots of storms this time of year."

"No, no, Kiss. It's not stormy at all. In fact, the weather is quite balmy. I wish you were here with me."

"I wish I were, too, honey. Next time, maybe, when you have a business trip to some exotic city, someplace really tropical. We can lie in bed with the palm trees wavin' outside the window, listenin' to the water slap up on the beach. Anyway, I'm sure you're havin' the best time, knowin' you."

"I'd be having a better time if you were with me."

"You're a sweet man, Monty. We'll have a good time when you get back, I promise."

"Kismet, I read a story about a sultan who was in love with a

slave girl, but the girl resisted him. Finally, he agreed that there
should be a scimitar between them in the bed, and..."

There was a loud knock on Monty's hotel room door, followed by a voice from the corridor.

"Mr. Rhodes! Mr. Rhodes, sir! Your guests are waiting."

"All right! I'll be right there!" Monty shouted. "Hello, Kiss,
I'm sorry, dear, I have to go. I hate to. I miss you."

"I miss you, too, Monty."

"Are you staying in tonight, dear? Have you plans?"

"No, no plans. You'd better go. Your guests are waiting."

"Good night, darling. I'll see you day after tomorrow."

"You'll tell me about the sultan and the scimitar."

"Oh, yes! I won't forget."

"Bye, love."

Monty hung up the telephone. He smelled something burning, looked down by his right foot and saw his cigaret boring a
hole in the carpet. He stepped on it.

Kismet lounged for a few moments on her bed, clad only in
panties and a short slip. She got up and walked over to a dresser where there was an uncapped bottle of tequila and a glass. She
poured a shot and drank it, then poured another and killed it in
two tries. She took the bottle back to the bed with her. Kismet
lay back and poured the tequila on her body, soaking her underwear, rubbing the alcohol into her breasts and stomach, massaging and stroking herself with one hand. The telephone rang
but Kismet ignored it. It kept ringing. Finally, she picked it up,

on perhaps the twentieth ring. She heard music, mournful, eerie strains made by a cello or bass viol. Kismet listened for a minute or two, then began to cry, softly at first, then harder. She dropped the telephone to the floor and continued to weep. Kismet could hear the strange music coming from the receiver. A voice shouted her name.

sweethearts

Sheriff Elihu Pitts drove along New Indianola Road singing his favorite song, "The Bonny Blue Flag," the original anthem of the Confederate States of America.

"First came South Carolina, which bravely took the stand," Pitts sang, then came Alabama, which took her by the hand. Then came Loozianna, and Mississippi, too. All hail the bonny blue flag that bears a single star. Hurrah—"

Just as the sheriff had begun the chorus, he heard a sharp rattling noise, and stopped singing. He heard it a second time, looked down, and saw coiled on the floor of the passenger side of his vehicle a diamondback rattlesnake. Pitts screeched the car to a stop and bolted out the driver's side door, rolling over several times on the side of the road until he was certain he was well out of striking range of the snake. He got up on one knee, unholstered his revolver and trained it on the vehicle. Pitts waited, sweating like a Djibouti bargeman. After a minute or two, the reptile appeared, depending from the driver's side floorboard until it sensed the earth and then slithered down onto the roadside, exposing its full six-and-a-half foot length and width the size of a large man's fist.

"Christ be a lady!" said Sheriff Pitts, just before he fired five rounds into or around the rattler's cranium, virtually decapitating it.

Following the adrenaline rush, a wave of nausea caused Pitts to vomit right where he knelt. When he had finished, the sheriff stood up, spat, and wiped tears from his eyes with his free hand. The air was windless, the early evening sky stained deep crimson. Pitts holstered his weapon, walked to the rear of his car, popped open the trunk, walked over and picked up what was left of the critter, walked back, tossed it into the trunk and closed it.

Within a half-mile, on Old Indianola Road, Webb Wirt sat on a pale blue inflatable armchair in the living room of his house. Webb Wirt was an obese, egg-shaped person, completely bald with large, elephantine ears. All of the furniture in his living room was blue and of an inflatable variety. Webb himself looked like an inflatable object. He was watching television, the blue light flickering in his face, and eating corn on the cob. After he finished an ear, Webb Wirt threw it onto the aqua linoleum floor, where it was nibbled at by hungry cats, of which Wirt kept dozens, all of them de-clawed so they would not rip and therefore deflate his inflatable furniture. Webb Wirt was laughing at the images on the television and tossing naked cobs to the cats when his buddy, Hubert Host, entered the house.

Hubert kicked corn and cats out of his way and deposited himself in a pale blue armchair identical to the one Webb sat in.

"What's on, Monkey?" asked Hubert.

"Old movie, one of my faves. One where this rich actress's maid's daughter passes herself off as white, then comes back for her mama's funeral years after runnin' out on her, and throws herself on the coffin, bawlin'. You prob'ly seen it. Lana Turner plays the actress, who's terrible and pretty dumb besides. Good castin', if you ask me. Only the Negro maid has an ounce of sense or goodness in her. You know, Yankee fag liberal shit. Us southern queens know better, don't we, Hube?"

"You bet, Webb."

"Where ya been?"

"Havin' dinner with Al Ball. He sends his regards."

"Speakin' of faggots!"

Both men laughed heartily.

"Good thing you ate, Hube. I pretty near finished all the corn."

Hubert got up and went into another room. He came back a minute later with a bottle of whiskey and two glasses, sat down and poured them each a healthy drink. Hubert handed one of the glasses to Webb.

"You're a sweetheart, Hube," he said. "Really you are."

the robbery

Just before hopping on her motorcycle, Trina Trübl planted a wet one flush on Billy Breaux's lips. As he reeled backwards from the

impact of her kiss, the Trübl sisters roared off into the night. Billy
was standing in their dust as Jack and Puma exited The Pharaoh's
Flame together.

"You comin' home with me?" she asked.

"I can't now, Poo," said Jack. "I'll be by later. I got some stuff
to take care of with Torch."

"See you whenever, then," Puma said, and kissed him. She
waved to Billy, got in her Dodge and drove away.

Billy, now mostly recovered from Trina's muscular osculation,
came over to Jack and shook his hand.

"That was sensational, son," said Billy. "You'n Jesse gonna
knock 'em dead."

Jack's half-smile went south. "Yes, sir," he said, "I guess we are."

Twenty minutes later, Jack and Jesse were in Torch Martin's
car, on their way to Webb Wirt's house. As Torch drove, Jesse
leaned over from the back seat and spoke rapidly in his strange
tongue to Jack.

"Can't you shut him up?" said Torch.

"Take it easy, Jess," Jack said, soothingly, and Jesse sat back.

"Now, I'm not plannin' on killin' him," Torch explained. "If he'll
cooperate, open up the safe and give us the money, he'll survive."

"What'll keep him from talkin', Torch? Can't imagine Webb
Wirt will be so easy to scare. He'll go straight to Al Ball."

"You'd be surprised sometimes, Jack, what a party'll do or
won't do. I know some secrets about him he won't want adver-
tised around Little Egypt."

"You mean him and Hubert Host? Shoot, everybody knows about them."

"He won't talk. I'll fix it. And if there's any doubts, well...let's just cross that river when we come to it."

Torch cut the headlights as he approached Webb Wirt's house and cruised slowly up the driveway.

"Look there," said Jack. "That's Hubert's car."

The lights were off in the house. Torch cut the engine.

"Maybe we ought to come back when Webb's alone."

"No," said Torch, "this is it, boys."

Torch took a gun from under the front seat and stuffed it into his jacket pocket. He smoothed back his long, dark red hair while looking in the rearview mirror. Jesse's permanent grin glared back at him.

"*Vamonos, compañeros!*" he said.

The trio got out of the car, being careful to quietly close the doors. They walked up to the house on cats' feet.

Torch pulled Jack and Jesse to him. "We'll go in through the same window we went in before."

"What about the python?" asked Jack.

"It ain't gonna bother us, I told you. If it does, shoot it."

"Me'n Jesse ain't got guns."

"Then wrestle the fucker to death, I don't care!"

They went directly to the basement window, Torch pried it open and motioned for Jesse to climb in first, followed by Jack. Torch pulled out a flashlight, which he shone through the opening.

As he went in, Jack said, "Show that beam, Torch. I don't want to step on no reptile!"

Torch jumped down and led the way as the three men crept through the eerie basement, mindful of the giant serpent lurking somewhere in the dark. They located the safe, then proceeded to the stairs leading up to the main part of the house.

"You two want to wait here, or come up?"

"You crazy?" said Jack. "We're all goin'."

Jack and Jesse followed Torch up the steps, through a door and into the kitchen. Torch flashed the light around, trying to figure out the lay of the land.

"I think the bedroom's this way," he said, and headed off.

They were in the living room when Jesse stepped on something that moved, then screeched.

"Goddamnit!" hissed Torch.

More screeches and yowls followed.

"What the hell's happening?!"

"Jesse stepped on a cat," Jack whispered.

The men hunkered down amidst the inflatable furniture and waited for the felines to settle down. Torch listened for signs that Webb and Hubert had been awakened by the cats, but no noises came from the direction of their bedroom. After a minute, Torch motioned them forward. They waited again near the open bedroom door, listening to the sleeping couple's snoring, gurgling, lip-slapping, turning, grunting, wind-breaking, teeth-gnashing and dream mumbling.

Torch walked into the bedroom and trained his flashlight beam on Webb and Hubert. Jack and Jesse followed him in. Both of the sleepers were completely naked, semi-covered by pale blue sheets on a waterbed. The intruders regarded with no small measure of disgust the piles of pink, lumpy flesh displayed on rumpled pale blue. Webb Wirt's nude dome gleamed in the yellow light. Hubert Host's hairy back contrasted dramatically with Webb's baby-like, butter-smooth torso.

"What now?" said Jack.

Torch moved closer to the sleepers and shined the light directly into Webb Wirt's face.

"Leap to it, maggots!" he shouted. "Rise and shine!"

Webb and Hubert knocked heads as they jumped up, pulling the covers over themselves.

Torch laughed. "You ladies looked so sweet lyin' there, it broke my heart to disturb y'all. But now that it's done, let's go to work."

"Martin!" Hubert Host shouted. "You deranged redneck! What is this?"

Torch held up his gun so that the men could see it.

"Expandin' bankin' hours, is what. Get your peachy self out of there, Mr. Wirt. Come on down to the basement with us."

Truly terrified, Webb Wirt shook as he asked, "What for?"

Hubert saw Jack and Jesse, and said to them, "Jack McDonald! Jesse! What's happening? What are you doing with this monster?"

"Don't bother these boys, Hubert," said Torch. "Your honeypie here cooperates, this won't take but a few minutes. You come, too. Get movin'!"

Webb and Hubert reluctantly obeyed Torch's orders, hurriedly pulling on their huge boxer shorts. They shuffled out of the bedroom ahead of Torch, Jack and Jesse.

The men proceeded Indian file through the living room, Torch and Jack kicking cats out of the way, into the kitchen and to the door leading to the basement.

Webb stopped. "Why do you want to go down there?" he asked.

"Why do you think?" said Torch. "Remember what Willie Sutton said when the cops asked him why he robbed banks?"

"No."

"'Cause that's where the money is."

"But I don't have any money!"

Torch herded Webb and Hubert down the stairs, he and the McDonald brothers following close behind. Hubert misstepped and fell, crashing into Webb, causing them to tumble headlong into the basement. They lay at the bottom of the stairs, groaning and moaning like two beached whales.

Torch clambered down after them and kicked at their bloated, oafish shapes, shouting, "Get up, you tubs of shit! Quit cryin'!"

When they were standing, Torch shone his beam on the safe.

"There's nothing in there!" Webb howled.

"Open it!"

"Noooooo!!!!!"

Hubert said, "You're a dead man if you do this, Martin."

"Hubert," said Torch, "you're a dead man whether you go along with us or not."

"Look, Torch," said Jack, "you're not gonna..."

"Take it easy, Jack. Let's just get what we come for. First things first, right? Come on, Webb, open it. Make everything flow."

Webb looked at Hubert.

"Go on, Webb," Hubert said, "better do what he says."

Webb whimpered and heaved, but he shuffled over to the safe and began turning the tumblers. There was a double click, and Webb stood back.

"I don't have the key," he said.

"Get it, then!" Torch said. "Where is it?"

"In a coffee can on the workbench. On the other side of the basement."

"Go get it."

"I need the light."

"Is there a light down here?" asked Torch. "Where's the switch?"

"There's a chain over there," said Hubert, pointing.

"Jesse! Jack! Get the light on!"

Jesse walked over to where the chain was, pulled it, then jumped away and yelled. The python was coiled up on the floor underneath the chain.

Hubert lunged for Torch's gun, but Torch saw him coming and whacked Host on the side of his head with it. The gun went off and all hell broke loose. Webb tried to escape up the stairs and Jack pulled him back down, wrestling the humpty-dumpty body to the floor. Torch and Hubert struggled for the gun and it went off again, this time discharging into Hubert's chest. The python slithered into the darkness as Jesse jumped up on top of a box to avoid both the snake and the line of fire.

Torch stood over Webb. "Get up, you sack of shit!"

Webb blubbered, rolled over, got to his knees. "Hube! Hube!" he cried. "Is he dead? Is Hubert dead?"

Everyone looked at Hubert Host. He was not breathing. There was a big red hole in his chest, out of which blood was spurting.

"Jesus, Torch," said Jack. "He is dead."

"Yeah. Get the key, Webb. Get the key and open up the cock-sucking safe! Now!"

"Oh, oh, Hube," Webb burbled. "Poor Hube."

He stood up, limped over to the workbench and pulled on a lightchain. Webb buried his right hand in a coffee can and came up with a small key. He limped to the safe and hesitated before inserting it into the lock, looking balefully at Jack.

"Go on, Mr. Wirt," Jack said. "Open it."

Webb turned the key in the lock, synchronized it with the combination, and swung open the twin doors of the old safe.

Torch rushed forward. "Jack! Jesse! Pull out the drawers!"

The brothers followed orders. In the vault drawers were two large canvas sacks filled with hundred dollar bills bound in packets of twenty each.

"I'll be damned," said Torch, inspecting the sacks and grinning from ear to ear. "For once I done somethin' right."

Webb Wirt began to wail and moan. His sobs became increasingly louder.

Torch put his left hand on the money in one of the sacks, and said, "Cut it out, Webb. Act like a man for a change."

Webb fell to his knees next to Hubert's corpse, his arms folded across his chest as he rocked back and forth, caterwauling.

"God damn!" yelled Torch, putting his hands to his ears. "Stop it!"

Webb raised his egg-shaped head, tears streaming down his face, and suddenly sprang at Torch, attacking him, knocking the gun away.

"Jack!" Torch shouted. "Get the gun!"

Webb's weight was too much for Torch to control easily. The half-naked Wirt rolled around on the floor with Torch, holding on to him as tightly as he could, attempting to smother him with his massive body. They crashed into a dark corner, the brothers staying out of it. Jesse spotted the gun, picked it up and handed it to Jack.

Suddenly, Webb let loose a horrible, bloodcurdling scream. Torch crawled out of the darkness toward the brothers. Jack and Jesse could see Webb's fat legs kicking in the air. Torch found the flashlight, turned back and directed it at Wirt's flailing limbs. The python had wrapped itself around Webb's neck and head and was squeezing him to death.

Jesse started babbling wildly and Jack comforted him, putting an arm around his brother's shoulders. Torch got to his feet and watched the snake crush its owner, listening to Webb's ribs and other bones crack. Finally, Webb vomited a white liquid and ceased his struggling. Torch walked over to the reptile and its prey.

"Bring me the gun, Jack," he said.

Jack handed it to him. Torch fired a bullet into the python's head, then another. A gaseous odor emanated from the entwined. Torch fired a round into Webb's heart.

"Just to make sure," said Torch. "Get this beast off him, boys."

Jack and Jesse attempted to unwrap the serpent, to pry it loose, but it was locked around Webb's body.

"Jesus, Torch, it's stuck on him."

Torch looked around the basement and came back with a machete. He handed it to Jack.

"Use this," he said.

Jack hacked away at the snake, managing to dislodge it at last. Blood and python guts littered the area. Jack stood up and stared at the disgusting mess.

"Should have let it eat him, maybe," said Torch.

"Huh?"

"Should have let the sucker devour ol' Webb. Then there wouldn'ta been no corpse to ditch."

"We'd still have had Hubert there."

Torch looked over at Hubert's remains and snorted. "Snake

mighta had him for dessert. Well, let's load 'em into the trunk of
the car. Go dump 'em in Ringtail Lake."

"What about the snake?" Jack asked.

"Leave it for the cats," said Torch. "They'll be gettin' hungry
soon."

dog and wolf

Torch Martin and the boys reached Ringtail Lake before sunrise,
during that curious hour between dog and wolf. Madrugada, the
Mexicans call it. Jack and Jesse removed the bodies one by one from
the trunk of the car, carried them the short distance to the lake,
then slid them into the water. Torch remained in the car behind the
steering wheel, observing the brothers as they did the dirty work.
The two canvas sacks filled with cash were piled next to him, on the
floor and on the front passenger seat. Torch had never been in pos-
session of so much money before and he needed to keep it close.
When the boys had finished depositing the bodies in the lake, Jack
shut the trunk lid and they climbed into the back seat.

"I guess that does it," said Jack.

"Hell of a night's work, men," said Torch. "Hell of an evening,
wasn't it?"

Torch gazed up at the strange, pink-black sky. "Look at that,
Jack, Jesse. Look at that sky. Almost makes you feel like you're on
another planet, or somethin'. Somethin' not quite real about it.
Like bein' on the edge of a cliff only you're upside down and
lookin' up but you could still fall off, you're not careful."

"Let's go, Torch. We're damn tired."

Torch laughed. "Yeah, I forgot you played a show last night, too. Great show, by the way. You boys is super already and gettin' better. Wouldn't be half-surprised if there's a bonus comin' up. Just to show my 'preciation of all your efforts, makin' the Flame such a success. What would y'all think of that?"

"That'd be good, Torch."

Torch started the car and rolled it slowly away from the lake. The sky came alive and a slight breeze rippled the water above Hubert and Webb's bodies.

At this moment, Puma twisted in her bed and opened her eyes. She sat up, wondering why Jack had not shown up as he said he would. She got out of bed, wearing only a T-shirt, picked up a package of cigarets from her night table, removed one, put it into her mouth, took a Bic lighter and fired up. Puma walked over to a window and stared out at the brightening sky.

Kismet's bedroom was a mess. All of the covers were on the floor, and she was spread-eagled on her stomach on the bed, completely nude, sound asleep. A radio was on, John Coltrane playing the ballad "Violets for Your Furs." The bedroom door opened slowly and Monty entered. He was wearing a Japanese kimono and his face was entirely white, covered with pancake makeup like a Geisha's. He mince-stepped silently over to the bed and bent over the body of his unconscious wife. Monty lay down, carefully, not wanting to rouse her. He lay perfectly still with his eyes open, listening to her breathing.

Mudcat, started awake by the noise of an automobile engine, looked out of a window by his bed and saw Torch's car drive by his cabin. Jack and Jesse were in the backseat.

Al Ball sat in a dark room, mopping his face with a rag. He was smoking a cigaret and holding a tall drink in his other hand. The radio was on, tuned to the same station as the radio in Kismet's bedroom. John Coltrane's tenor saxophone played beautifully, softly. Al Ball listened intently, patting gently at his impossibly wet cheeks and chin.

Billy Breaux coughed himself awake in his bed. He coughed and coughed until he expectorated a throatful of phlegm into a handkerchief. He reached for a pack of cigarets next to his bed, lit one, inhaled, then coughed some more. Billy cleared his throat and sat quietly on the edge of his bed, smoking as light snuck into his room.

Sheriff Pitts' patrol car was parked outside his house, the sheriff half-awake in the front seat. He could hear the sounds of a woman inside, crying.

the morning after, the day before

Puma's battered Dodge stealthily negotiated the tricky, rough road to Jack and Jesse's cabin. She drove up to the front of it and parked, got out, walked up to the door and knocked. When there was no response, she knocked harder. Finally, Jack opened the door.

"Hi, Poo," he said, his eyes half-closed from sleep, "come on in."

Puma entered and asked, "What happened last night, Jack?"

"What do you mean, what happened?"

Jesse yawned audibly from his bed, which was in the front room of the cabin, where Jack and Puma were talking.

"Mornin', Jesse," she said.

He nodded, grinned, got up and padded off to the bathroom.

"You said you were gonna come by, after your business with Torch."

"Oh, I'm sorry, sweetheart. It just took longer than I thought it would. Then both Jess and I were so beat from the gig and all, we just conked out. I shoulda called, though, I guess. How's your dad?"

Jack cuddled her.

"Same. No better, no worse. It's how he'll be 'til he's gone, doc says. I just missed you last night, Jack. I had a bad time."

"I didn't sleep so well, either."

Jesse came out of the bathroom, hurriedly pulled on pants, shirt and shoes, grinned at the couple, and left the cabin. He walked down the road toward the Flame, which was only a few hundred yards away. As he approached the roadhouse, he saw Ralphie shove Mudcat. Jesse hurried over, talking his talk.

Ralphie spotted Jesse coming at him.

"Stay out of this, dummy," he yelled. "It ain't your affair."

"It's okay, Jesse," said Mudcat. "I can handle this punk."

Ralphie turned viciously on Mudcat, spitting out his words.

"Nigger, you keep your nose out of my business!"

Jesse jumped Ralphie and threw him to the ground, strad-
dling Torch's flunky, beating on him, landing solid punches so
rapidly and furiously that Ralphie quickly submitted.

"Stop! Stop!" he cried. "I give up!"

Jesse slowly withdrew, but remained standing over him.
Ralphie started to talk but Jesse pointed a finger at him and he
shut up. Ralphie lay still on the ground, and when Jesse was satisfied that he would not move again until allowed to do so, Jesse
moved away. He and Mudcat walked together toward the Flame.

Inside the roadhouse, Torch was on the telephone.

"Sure, Kiss, I will. They'll be fine. I got cabins for 'em. Uh
huh. I'll do everything I can for 'em, baby, just like I do for you."
Torch laughed. "Okay, Kiss, I'll see you later."

Torch hung up, and said, "Christ, a bughouse choir!"

He picked up the phone again and dialed a number.

"This is Torch Martin. I'd like to speak with Mr. Ball. Yeah,
I'll hold for a second. Mr. Ball! Al! Yes, yes. Say, I have a deliv-
ery for you. I know it's a little late, but I got it. I wanted to make
sure this is a good time for my man to bring it over. It is? Great,
great. You'll have it right quick, then, Mr. Ball. Al! All of it, yes,
sir. Plus the interest, right. Hubert? No, I haven't seen him. I
will, yes. Yes. All right, then. My pleasure, Al. And thank you,
sir. You bet. Oh, no. I know you don't! Just a habit of speech, uh
huh. Bye now, uh, Al."

Torch hung up, stood, and went to the door of his office.

"Dogeyes!" he shouted. "Come in here!"

Dogeyes entered Torch's office. Torch picked up a leather suit-case and put it into Dogeyes's hand.

"Take this down to Al Ball's place. Get Ralphie to go along with you. Hand it to Ball himself, nobody else. Got that?"

"I hand it to Mr. Ball, nobody else."

Dogeyes walked out of the office, followed by Torch. Jesse and Mudcat were sitting at the bar, drinking coffee and eating doughnuts. Torch watched Dogeyes leave, then glanced over at Mudcat and Jesse.

"How you doin', boys?"

"We doin' what we like, and we like what we doin', Mr. Martin."

Torch came over to them. "Don't you wish the whole world was that way, Mudcat? Listen, there's gonna be some women arrivin' in a little while, and I want you to make sure they're taken care of right."

"Girls from Oriental."

"That's right. Mrs. Rhodes is gonna be here to help 'em set up. Jesse, I guess you and Jack are gonna provide the backup."

Jesse nodded and smiled.

"Well," said Torch, "it'll be somethin' different for the Flame."

"Be a big success, I think," said Mudcat. "Not many folks in Little Egypt ever seen a group of crazy women sing. Least not certified crazy."

"That's for certain."

"I guess every kind of thing come through Little Egypt

sooner or later, Mr. Martin. I'm sure it gon' be a unique experience for us all."

"Mudcat, I'm sure it will."

Torch went back into his office and closed the door.

the eyes have it

Dogeyes and Ralphie entered Al Ball's office. Edgar took the leather suitcase from Dogeyes and motioned for the two men to sit down in chairs in front of Ball's desk. Al was seated directly across from them. Edgar put the suitcase on the desk.

"No, Edgar!" Al Ball shouted. "Not on the desk! Take it over in the corner there, open it up and count it."

Edgar removed the suitcase.

"Thank you," said Al Ball. "Now, gentlemen, while Edgar makes certain all is in order, we'll chat. Would you like a drink? A cigaret?"

"No, sir," said Dogeyes. "Thanks."

"No, thank you, Mr. Ball," Ralphie followed.

"You're the one they call Dogeyes, right?"

"Yes, sir."

"Why is that?"

"It's because of my strabismus, I guess. I got, my right eye, it kind of goes the wrong way. It diverges from the other one. It's called a strabismus, the condition."

"A walleye, you mean," said Al. "It's a walleye."

"Yeah, a walleye. Also, I'm color blind."

"So, you're walleyed and color blind. Why aren't you called Walleye, then?"

"Because of dogs are supposed to be color blind."

Al Ball mopped his runny face with a bright pink hanky. His epidermal discharges left brown stains on the cloth.

"We most of us have one or more infirmities we have to live with," Al Ball said, "to adjust to. We do it, right, Dogeyes? In terms of who we are inside, external lesions or malformations are not really critical to our existence."

"No, sir."

"They do inform our character, however, do you agree? Dogeyes, do you agree?"

"Ah, yes. Yes, sir, I do."

"What's your real name? Your Christian name."

"Jerome."

"All right, Jerome. And Ralphie, do you?"

"Do I?" said Ralphie.

"Agree," said Al Ball.

"Uh, yeah, yeah. I agree."

"How you doin' over there, Edgar?"

"Almost done, boss. Looks like it's all here."

"Includin' the interest?"

"Gimme another minute."

"Wounds," said Al Ball, "scars, infirmities. If a person accepts them for what they are his reward is strength of character. Ralphie, would you say Dogeyes—Jerome—here, exemplifies this?"

"Uh, sure, Mr. Ball. He's real strong. Definitely a strong person." Ralphie laughed. "I like to have him on my side in a fight."

Edgar shut the suitcase, snapped the locks down, brought it over and set it down next to the desk.

"It's all here, Mr. Ball."

Al Ball wiped and stared at the two men seated in front of him.

"Have either of you seen Hubert Host today?"

"No, sir," said Dogeyes.

"Uh, no," said Ralphie.

"Fair enough, then, gentlemen. Tell Mr. Martin this matter is at rest. Show them out, Edgar."

Edgar opened the door. "Let's go, boys," he said.

The men left and Edgar closed the door.

"Edgar, where is Hubert? Have you called Webb Wirt's house?"

"No answer."

Al Ball stood up. "We'll take a ride out to Webb's. Somethin's not right."

Kismet sat at the dressing table in her bedroom, putting on makeup, clad only in bra and panties, when Monty entered.

"Hi, Monty," she said. "I'm just gettin' ready to go over by the Flame. The girls from Oriental oughta be pullin' in any time now."

Monty, dressed carefully in a gray suit, stood behind his wife, watching her apply eyeliner.

"Kismet, you know I love you very much."

"'Course, darlin'. I love you very much, too."

Finished with her eyes, Kismet got up and began putting on the stockings, skirt and blouse she had laid out on her bed.

Monty watched her intently. "I don't know how I could live without you," he said.

"Well, you don't need to be worryin' over that. I ain't goin' anywhere."

"It might be me, Kiss. It might be me who would go somewhere. Did that thought ever occur to you?"

"Monty, I don't know what's festerin' in that little brain of yours, but I kind of have my thoughts trained on this evenin' right now. Where you thinkin' on goin'? You just got back from Birmingham, and a day early at that."

"I missed you terribly. I needed to see you. I was pleased to find you at home."

"Where else would I be in the middle of the night, Monty? I'm just your average American wife, passed out from drinkin' too much tequila, waitin' on my man."

"You wouldn't do anything to embarrass me, would you, Kismet? Embarrass my family?"

"Such as?"

Monty is sweating heavily, visibly. "T-t-t-torch Martin. Ha-ha-have you been s-s-s-seeing Torch Martin?"

Finished dressing, Kismet stood up and looked directly into her husband's eyes.

"I see him when I'm at The Pharaoh's Flame, of course. He's

agreed to have the Oriental girls perform there, as you know. That's all."

"That's all."

"Yes, Monty, that's all. Now, I gotta go."

Kismet kissed Monty on his right cheek, as a mother would. She picked up her purse and car keys.

"You'll be by tonight to see us, won't you?"

"I'll be there," said Monty.

"Eight o'clock. Love you," she said, and left Monty alone in the room.

Immediately after Kismet walked out, Monty felt a horrible pain in his stomach and doubled over, dropping to his knees next to the bed.

the devil in disguise

Two vans strained up the road to The Pharaoh's Flame. On the sides of each van was painted: "SHE HATH A DEVIL, AND IS MAD; WHY HEAR YE HER?"—JOHN 10:20. Women were hanging out of the windows, dust from the road billowing up around their faces. Each van was driven by a large, broad-shouldered woman wearing a green uniform and matching baseball cap with the letters OSI sewn above the bill. The vehicles reached the roadhouse and stopped. The doors swung open and the passengers disembarked in a rush.

The women ranged in age from fifteen to thirty-five, and each of them carried a small overnight case. Many of them seemed confused; others flitted around like bumblebees, giggling, hopping up and down, delighted and frightened at the same time. The drivers and two other similarly built and garbed women worked to gather the others together. The last person to disembark from the second van was a very small, Asian woman, who made her presence known by blowing a whistle attached to a string around her neck.

"Ladies! Ladies!" the small woman shouted. "Line up! Line up! We must make order!"

As the tiny Asian woman and her four burly helpers attempted to organize their flock, Torch Martin, accompanied by Mudcat, came out of the Flame to greet them.

The Asian woman approached Torch, and asked, "You are Mr. Martin?"

"Yes, that's me. I'm the proprietor of The Pharaoh's Flame here, where you'll be performin'."

The woman grabbed Torch's right hand in her own and gripped it tightly.

"My name is Imelda Go," she said, "artistic and creative director of the Oriental State Institute. We are so pleased, Mr. Martin, so very, very pleased to be here, to be able to perform for your community of Little Egypt. It will be an event your community will not soon forget, I assure you. The girls and I have labored, labored very hard, these past few weeks."

As Imelda Go spoke, some of the girls were getting out of hand behind her, running away from the attendants, who chased after them.

Kismet Rhodes drove up in her sleek car. She got out and came over to Torch and Imelda.

"Yes, Miss Go," said Torch, wrenching his hand out of Imelda's as soon as he spotted Kismet, "here's Mrs. Rhodes now."

"Hello, Imelda, darlin'!" Kismet said. "So good y'all made it!"

The two women kissed each other on the cheek and hugged. One of the Oriental attendants grabbed Mudcat and pushed him off in the direction of a couple of wandering women.

"Mrs. Rhodes," said Imelda, "the girls are so excited! This is a big moment in their lives."

"Torch," Kismet said, "I hope you won't regret this. You can see how much it means to the women here."

Torch watched the antics of the women, and said, "I got an open mind, Kiss, you know that. Miss Imelda, we got some cabins prepared for your group. They're just up this way, on the other side of the Flame."

"Are Jack and Jesse and the band here?" asked Kismet.

"I seen 'em a few minutes ago, settin' up inside. Hey, Mudcat! Mudcat! Where'd he go? Come on, Miss Imelda, I'll show y'all to the cabins myself, if you can gather the ladies."

"Thanks, Torch," said Kismet. "You know how much your doin' this means to me."

Imelda Go went after one of the girls.

"I sure do, honey," said Torch. "Why don't you go on in and check on Jack and Jesse? I'll take care of gettin' the girls settled in."

Kismet kissed Torch on the cheek. "You're a strange guy, Torch. Sometimes you can be a real angel."

"Go on, Kiss. I'll see you inside."

the nature of the beast

Al Ball and Edgar drove down Old Indianola Road toward Picnic Hill through a fine late afternoon mist. Edgar, who was behind the wheel of Al Ball's black Lincoln Town Car, switched on the windshield wipers.

"You ever wonder, Edgar, why anybody sticks it out here in the middle of Mississippi?"

"It's where they live."

"Weather's bad and the people go from bad to worse. Enough of 'em, anyway."

"Plenty of good lookin' women, though," said Edgar.

Al Ball sucked on the unlit stub of a Macanudo.

"Go along with you there, scout," he said, staring out at the scenery. "Plus, country like this, always places to stash a body."

As they approached Picnic Hill, the men saw Hubert's Crown Victoria sedan parked in front of Webb Wirt's house.

"Somethin's not right is right," Al Ball said. "Edgar, this don't smell good."

Edgar pulled the Lincoln next to the Ford, killed the engine, and the men got out. They walked up to the front door and Edgar knocked on it. There was no response, so he knocked again, harder. Al Ball looked around.

"Kick it in, Edgar. Kick in the door."

Edgar kicked it open and the two men entered the house. Several cats dodged them as they walked through the room filled with inflatable blue furniture.

"Edgar, you been in here before?"

"No, boss, I ain't."

"A normal person don't live like this."

They continued through the house, scattering cats as they went, checking each room. In the master bedroom, they saw an unmade bed, men's clothing strewn on the floor and over chairs. Cats slept on the waterbed. Al and Edgar came to the door to the basement, which was wide open. They peered down the stairway. Al Ball mopped his face. Edgar found a lightswitch and flicked it on, illuminating the stairway.

"We goin' down there, boss?"

"You first."

Edgar led the way. At the bottom of the stairs they saw the safe, its doors spread. Edgar went over and stood next to a man-sized bloodstain on the floor. Light streamed in from the windows and two hanging bulbs were lit.

"Somethin' happened here, all right," said Edgar. "This ain't paint."

Al Ball waved his handkerchief. "Over there. Look over there."

The two men walked toward the far side of the basement. A dozen or more cats were eating the hacked up parts of the python. Drunk on snakemeat and blood, the felines tore and licked at their grisly repast in a frenzy, like hyenas diving into the anus and large intestine of a freshly slaughtered cape buffalo. The collective purr of the voracious cats made a humming sound similar to that of a power generator.

"Boss, that's not them, is it? Hubert and Webb?"

"No," said Al Ball. "Look there."

He pointed to the severed python head with bullet holes in it.

"That's the head of the rest of it, whatever it was. This was not human."

"What about Hubert and Webb?"

"I think I know, Edgar. Come on, this place stinks."

The men made their way back up the stairs, the droning noise of ravenous felines in their ears.

take it to the bank

Monty entered the outer office of his father, Montgomery Rhodes, Senior, owner of Rhodes Industries, which included the local refinery, the largest employer in Palestine County.

"Why, hi there, Junior," said a secretary. "You come to see your father?"

"Hello, Lucy. Yes, I had a message that he wanted me to come in."

"I'll just buzz him. How's your lovely Kismet?"

"Getting lovelier, thanks. She's singing tonight at The Pharaoh's Flame with women from Oriental. I'm on the board of the Institute."

Lucy spoke into the intercom. "Mr. Rhodes, your son is here. Yes, sir."

She looked up at Monty and said, "You can go right in, Junior. I'll be there tonight. I can't wait."

"Thanks, Lucy."

Monty entered his father's office and saw him shooting pool by himself. Rhodes, Senior, was sixty years old, tall and raw-boned, a Gary Cooper type, only less handsome. He had built his business from the ground up and still looked as if he could pull a twelve-hour shift at the refinery. He banked a shot and walked rapidly around the table, eager to keep his run of balls going.

"Sit down, Junior. I'll talk while I shoot."

Monty sat in a chair. "What's this about, Dad? Is there a problem?"

"If there is, you'll have to solve it."

"Is it about Birmingham? I thought everything went well. Biller agreed to the pricing changes, and..."

"Damn! Almost had a double-bank in the side pocket! No, Junior, it's not about Birmingham. It's about Kismet."

Monty felt his stomach cramp. He bent over slightly in pain.

"Little Egypt is a small town, son," Rhodes, Senior, said, oblivious to Monty's discomfort, "relatively speaking. When Paul the Apostle preached to the Corinthians in 50 A.D., he confronted a city noted for everything depraved, dissolute, and debauched. That ain't the case here. Somebody wants to do something out of the ordinary, better they go to Memphis or

Nashville or Chicago to do it. Otherwise, word gets passed around faster than jumper cables at a nigger funeral."

Rhodes, Senior, stuck the five in a far corner, putting enough english on the cueball to allow for an easy follow-up of the one in the side. He stood back from the table for a moment and noticed Monty's grimace.

"You all right, boy?"

"Yes, yes, I'm okay," said Monty, sweating now. "What about Kismet?"

"She has your name, son. My name. She is Mrs. Montgomery Rhodes, Junior, and she's draggin' it around in the mud."

Monty bent forward again. He was in terrible pain.

"Dad, I..."

"This is not the old days, Junior, where I could just make a man disappear and nobody would ask any questions. No, this is a different world. God damn it! Just once I'd like to massé a shot the way Willie Mosconi could."

Rhodes, Senior, stalked the table, lining up his next shot.

"No, son, you'll have to control your own wife. You understand this? You know what I'm talkin' about? Do you?"

"Yessss," hissed Monty. He was close to collapse.

"All right, then. The Rhodes name means a lot in this county, in this state. Hell, it means somethin' in the goddamn U.S. Congress!"

He looked at his son. "You need some Pepto? Go ask Lucy for some Pepto."

"Sure, Dad."

Monty managed to rise and walk out of the office.

"You're a Rhodes!" his father shouted. "A Rhodes takes care of his own business!"

Rhodes, Senior, banked a long, difficult shot.

"Yes!" he said.

quartet

Puma sat at her father's bedside. The shades were drawn, keeping the room in almost total darkness. She was holding his hand when life passed out of him, and she clearly heard his death rattle, a quiet, choking gurgle. Puma kissed his hand and held it against her cheek.

Monty sat in the men's room at Rhodes Industries. He was in a stall with the door locked, on the toilet, sobbing.

At Sheriff Pitts's house all of the curtains were closed. Edna Pitts, the sheriff's wife, was curled up on the floor of the living room, directly below her husband's dangling legs. The sheriff was hanging by the neck from a chandelier, twisting slowly. His widow sobbed in a fetal posture, her eyes closed. Suddenly, the fixture dislodged from the ceiling, the weight of the sheriff's body ripping it out of its mooring. Elihu Pitts, attached to the chandelier and a heavy chunk of plaster, crashed down on the prone Edna.

Al Ball and Edgar drove on a dirt road to Ringtail Lake. Up ahead, they saw a man waving to them. Edgar stopped the Lincoln next to the man, and they got out of the car. The man, who was dressed like a farmer, clad in bib overalls and a Caterpillar Tractor hat, pointed at the lake. Close to shore where the three men stood floated two grotesquely bloated corpses, fish nibbling at them from below. Next to the lake stood a plow horse with a halter, heavy rope and hook hanging from its neck. The horse's mane ruffled in the breeze, its brown coat matted from the steady, fine rain. Al and Edgar turned back to the car.

tough call

Jack and Jesse were on the stage at The Pharaoh's Flame with their band, rehearsing arrangements for that evening's perform-ance, when Billy Breaux entered. He spotted the boys on the bandstand and went over to them.

"Jack, Jesse, how y'all doin'? Look, I know you guys are busy here, but I just wanted to see you before I take off."

"We appreciate your comin' all this way to hear us, Mr. Breaux," said Jack.

Billy handed him a card. "Here's my address and phone number in Nashville. I'm on my way there now. You fellas con-tact me whenever you're ready. There's no doubt in my mind we can take the cake."

Jack smiled through his perpetual scowl. "We're pleased to hear you say that, sir."

"Billy."

"Okay, Billy. Too bad you can't stick around for the fireworks tonight. It's gonna be somethin' different, though we ain't sure just how."

Billy laughed. "I'm sure it will be, but I've got to be in Nashville before mornin'. You boys take good care, now. Don't forget Billy Breaux!"

"No, sir, we sure won't."

Billy shook hands with Jack and then with Jesse before departing. Mudcat came running in as Billy walked out and came up to Jack.

"Jack, there's a phone call for you. Torch says to take it in his office."

"Thanks, Mudcat. Back in a minute, Jesse."

Jack jumped down from the stage and went into Torch's office. Torch motioned for Jack to pick up the phone, which was lying on the desk, off the hook. Jack lifted the receiver to his ear.

"This is Jack McDonald."

He listened for a few moments before sitting down.

"Oh, Poo, I'm sorry, honey," Jack said. "Yes, yes, it was. You and your mama all right? Can Jesse and I do anything? No, I don't expect so. We're about to rehearse. Okay, honey. I love you."

Jack hung up the phone.

"Bad news, huh?" asked Torch.

"Puma's daddy died. He'd been ailin' for some time. Passed in his sleep."

"He's luckier'n most, wouldn't you say? Oh, Jack, I got yours and your brother's shares from the other night sorted out. You know, that bonus I mentioned? You want it now or you like me to keep it for you in the office safe here?"

Jack scowled even more darkly than usual. "We don't want nothin' of it, Torch. If you hadn't been holdin' things over my head, I never woulda gone along. Now we're quits. We're even."

Torch sat back in his chair and smiled. "That's the way you see it?"

Jack stood up. "That's the way it is."

"Okay, Jack, it's your call."

"Consider it made," Jack said, and walked out.

either/or

Inside Webb Wirt's house, the cats continued their picnic in the basement. Upstairs, they cavorted, cleaned themselves and rested on and amidst the inflatable blue furniture.

Montgomery Rhodes, Junior, sat on his bed in his house carefully loading a gun, polishing each bullet with a silk handkerchief before inserting it into the weapon. Tears streamed down his face as he listened at full volume to a recording of Maria Callas singing Elizabeth's aria from Don Carlo.

In the inner office of Montgomery Rhodes, Senior, Lucy lay spread-eagled on the pool table, her dress up around her waist. The senior Rhodes dropped his trousers and climbed on top of his secretary, knocking away the poolballs as he did so. The radio was turned up loud as Jimi Hendrix sang, "Is this love, baby...or is it confusion?"

Out the window of the office was a magnificent view of smoke rising from the refinery into the darkening skies over Little Egypt. The sunset was bloody, horribly beautiful as pollutants from the smokestacks mixed with the gathering clouds and fading light.

The Pharaoh's Flame had been transformed from a roadhouse into a theater by the time of that evening's performance. A curtain was drawn across the stage and chairs had been brought in and set up on the dancefloor. Dogeyes, Ralphie and Mudcat were at the door collecting money from patrons as they arrived. Virtually the entire population of Little Egypt had been drawn to the event.

Torch stood to the side near the entrance, watching the people flow in and take their seats. He wore a new suit for the occasion, feeling especially flush and good about himself now that his debts were paid and he was doing something special for Kismet.

The Trübl sisters entered, dressed in fancy leathers, wearing high heels and causing more than their usual stir. The Flame was filling up fast, leaving standing room only.

Backstage, Imelda Go blew her whistle and gathered her girls together. The Oriental women were attired in antebellum costumes with which they could not stop fussing. Jack and Jesse and their bandmates wore tuxedos provided by Torch Martin. Kismet had on a gold lamé dress like Rita Hayworth's in Gilda. She was breathtakingly beautiful on this night, and she knew it. Kismet did her best to assist Imelda Go in controlling the nervous singers, who could not stop jostling, pulling and pushing one another as they endeavored to assume their proper places.

Out front, Monty entered the Flame and took a seat in the front row that had been reserved for him. He seemed calm, nodding and responding with his customary courtesy to the citizens of Little Egypt.

Lucy, Monty's father's secretary, arrived with a date, appearing exceptionally buoyant as they took their seats. They were followed closely by Mr. and Mrs. Montgomery Rhodes, Senior, Little Egypt's leading citizens. Rhodes, Senior, nodded and smiled at Lucy as he and his wife took their seats.

As the lights dimmed, Torch stood in the back, as did Dogeyes, Ralphie and Mudcat. A spotlight fell on center stage, the curtains parted, and Kismet stepped forward. The audience applauded at the sight of her.

"Honey, you look gooood!" shouted Trina Trübl.

"Ladies and gentlemen of Little Egypt and Palestine County," said Kismet, "thank you so very much for attending this first public performance of the women of Oriental, known beginning tonight as The Orientalites. Performing with them will be your own Jack and Jesse McDonald and the Flaming Band, as will I."

The audience applauded and whistled at this news.

"Thank you. I hope y'all will feel the same way when we're done. Before we begin, I want to especially thank Ms. Imelda Go, the artistic director of Oriental, who is responsible for bringin' the women here tonight. Come on out here a moment, Imelda, let me show you off."

Imelda Go stepped out from the wing and took a short bow, then quickly withdrew, as the audience politely applauded.

"Finally," Kismet announced, "both Imelda and I owe a debt of gratitude to the owner and operator of The Pharaoh's Flame, Mr. Torch Martin, for allowin' us to do this. Thanks a bunch, Torch."

After the audience's applause for Torch had died down, Imelda Go blew her whistle and the Orientalites took the stage.

During the performance, after Torch assured himself that things were going smoothly, he went outside in front of the Flame to smoke a cigaret. As he stood there, smoking, Al Ball's black Lincoln pulled up. Torch went over and leaned his head in the open rear window.

"Hey, Al. You're late. The show's already on."

"I couldn't make it, Torch," said Al Ball, who sat on the far side of the back seat, away from Torch. "And, thanks to you, neither could Webb or Hubert."

Torch dropped his cigaret. "Look, Al…"

"No, Torch," said Al Ball, bringing up a gun, "you look."

Al Ball shot Torch point blank in the face. Torch fell backward and then went down.

"Drive, Edgar," Al Ball said.

Inside the Flame, Monty was sweating like crazy. He was fighting the urge to double over from his stomach pain, trying not to draw attention to himself. Finally, when he could no longer stand it, as Kismet stepped to the edge of the stage to sing, Monty stood, took out his pistol and shot her. As everyone in the Flame reacted, screaming and shouting, Monty moved forward to fire again. Jesse jumped in front of Kismet just as Monty pulled the trigger a second time, taking the slug meant for her. Monty then turned the gun on himself and put a bullet into his brain.

The Pharaoh's Flame was in chaos. The audience stormed the door, desperate to get out, and onstage the Oriental women were howling in terror. Jack bent over both Kismet and Jesse. For once, Jesse was not grinning.

"Jack, I...I...I'm all right," said Jesse, speaking for the first time in a normal voice. "H-h-help Kiss."

Jack looked at Kismet and saw a red-black stream running from her left eye.

"It's too late, Jess," he said.

On the floor in front of the stage, Montgomery Rhodes, Senior, knelt, holding in his arms his son's limp body. His wife had passed out in her seat.

lost and found

Jack's pickup truck was parked in front of The Pharaoh's Flame, loaded with all of his and Jesse's belongings. Parked next to it was Puma's Dodge, also loaded, with gear strapped to the roof. Jack, Puma and Jesse, his left arm in a sling, stood together with Mudcat under an overcast sky.

"Y'all knock 'em out in Nashville, hear?" said Mudcat. "I'll be listenin'."

Jack smiled at him. "We'll do it, Cat. We'll do it."

Jack climbed into his truck and Puma got into her car. Jesse stood and grinned at Mudcat, who grinned back. They shook hands, then Jesse hopped into the passenger side of the pickup. Jack and Puma fired up their vehicles and headed down the road.

Suddenly, Puma spun a yo-yo and drove back up to the Flame, stopping in front of Mudcat. She grinned at him. He opened the passenger side door of the Dodge and got in.

Barry Gifford's novels have been translated into twenty-two languages. His book *Night People* was awarded the Premio Brancati in Italy, and he has been the recipient of awards from PEN, the National Endowment for the Arts, the American Library Association, and the Writers Guild. David Lynch's film based on Gifford's novel *Wild at Heart* won the Palme d'Or at the Cannes Film Festival in 1990, and Barry Gifford's novel *Perdita Durango* was made into a feature film in 1997. Gifford co-wrote with director David Lynch the film *Lost Highway*, also released in 1997. His most recent books include *The Phantom Father: A Memoir* (named a *New York Times* Notable Book of the Year); and *Wyoming*, a novel (named a Best Novel of the Year by the *Los Angeles Times*), which has been adapted for the stage and film.

Gifford lives in the San Francisco Bay area.

For more information, please visit www.barrygifford.com.